"I came to give you Nick. He's... your son."

Alessandro kept his voice low, but it still bit. "Are you trying to tell me that you and I were lovers?" His laugh held a harsh edge. "There isn't a chance that once I'd had you in my bed I'd forget such a memorable occasion."

Lauren's gaze fastened on him for an endless moment and he felt as if she were searching for something deep within him.

"So when and where was he conceived?" Alessandro's mouth twisted. "And perhaps I should ask...with whom?"

Dear Reader

Christmas is my favourite time of the year. It's a time for joy and laughter as much as it's a time for stories that touch the heart. It's also a time for miracles. The miracle of love. The miracle of family...

THE BABY GIFT is a deeply emotional story about a woman who knows she can't take care of the baby in her custody by herself, even though she wants to keep the child with every particle of her being. And it's the story of a man who learns to accept, love, and cherish THE BABY GIFT he's given—and the very special woman who presents him with this gift.

I hope you enjoy my latest book, and I wish you and yours true happiness this holiday, along with health, peace, and a New Year filled with joyful memories.

Love

Day Leclaire

P.S. As for the bathtub scene—it really happened. To me, unfortunately!

THE BABY GIFT

BY
DAY LECLAIRE

To Dee Tenorio.
Many, many thanks for sharing baby Gio with me!
You're the greatest.

First published in Great Britain 2000
Harlequin Mills & Boon Limited,
Eton House, 18-24 Paradise Road, Richmond, Surrey TW9 1SR

© Day Totton Smith 2000

ISBN 0 263 82113 7

Set in Times Roman 10½ on 12 pt.
02-1200-44769

Printed and bound in Spain
by Litografia Rosés, S.A., Barcelona

PROLOGUE

Ten days before Christmas…

SHE came to him again, all silk and sweetness and heady feminine perfume. Everything about her was soft—from her hip-length cornsilk hair, to her gentle, eager touch, to her soothing words. And her mouth… Her warm, hungry, giving mouth was softest of all.

She flowed over him, rousing emotions he thought had been gutted long ago. He was helpless to resist. Hell, resistance was the furthest thing from his mind. He wanted her. Needed her.

Took her.

Alessandro awoke with a jolt.

Tossing back his covers, he escaped the rumpled bed and crossed to stare out at a star-studded winter sky. Why did that dream continue to haunt him? It was so nebulous, so lacking in form or substance. And yet, it filled him with an odd restlessness. There was something he'd forgotten to do. Something urgent.

But he couldn't remember what.

He reached for the chain and ring that encircled his neck, cursing when he didn't find it. He'd lost it almost two years ago, and normally, he remembered that. But on the odd occasion—frustrating occasions when his emotions got the better of him—he reverted

5

to a habit that had been established in boyhood, when the chain had first been placed around his neck by his grieving father.

It was because of his dream, he acknowledged, a dream that had been haunting him with increasing regularity for the past nine months. The woman in it was, without question, his ex-wife, though for some reason Rhonda's hair was longer and silkier than the flaming red corkscrew curls that had rioted around her face during their eighteen months together. And while he wanted his ex with a painful desperation while asleep, when he woke he couldn't find the tiniest ember of passion lingering from the disaster of their marriage and subsequent divorce.

Pain, sure. Anger, definitely. Regrets, plenty. But there wasn't a shred of love or desire. He leaned his arm against the casing of the bay window, his hand folding into a fist. So why the dreams? And what the hell was he supposed to do? What had he forgotten?

"Come on, Salvatore. *Think.*"

The melancholy hoot of a great horned owl escaped from the California woods surrounding the family's mountain cabin, the sound a painful echo of his own loneliness. He hated this time of year. Or perhaps he just hated the memories it roused. Drawing back from the window, he glared at the dream-tossed bed, his frustration mounting.

What the hell had he forgotten?

CHAPTER ONE

Seven days before Christmas...

SHE *came to him again, all silk and sweetness and heady feminine perfume. There was a uniqueness to her that he instantly recognized, even in his dreams. It was as though they both sang the same song, their voices perfectly pitched to one another. He could hear his own laughter melding with hers, just as their bodies had melded throughout their long nights together. And then she whispered something to him as she danced through drifts of powder-soft snow, something he strained to hear. But the words escaped into the frigid night air before he could catch them. He swung her in his arms before she escaped, too, and the scene changed.*

They were no longer outside in the snowy coldness, but in the bedroom they'd shared for eighteen short months. He dropped her to the bed, her long cornsilk hair splaying across the pillow in streams of vibrant red. She said something to him again, but he still couldn't hear. She smiled in gentle understanding, a smile he'd never before seen on his wife's lush mouth. He approached, drawn by the warmth of her regard and the sweet promise in her hazel eyes.

He was helpless to resist. He wanted her. Needed her. Took her.

*   *   *

The harsh bark of an ax biting wood joined with the relentless shriek of the snow-laden wind. Alessandro paused in his exertions long enough to slant a quick upward glance toward the roiling sky. It wouldn't be long before snow began to fall in earnest. Already fat flakes drifted earthward. He shifted restlessly, plagued by the remnants of what had become an ongoing dream. Or perhaps he should call it a nightmare. It came closer to describing the choked, desperate sensations each incident stirred. Worse, he couldn't seem to escape them. His grip tightened on the ax handle and he swore beneath his breath.

Why now? It had been two full years, dammit. Why after all this time had memories of Rhonda returned to haunt him? Sweat dripped into his eyes, despite the piercing rawness of the wind, and he shook his hair back from his brow, regarding the felled tree he'd been chopping with renewed determination. With luck, he could drive out the demons haunting him with some plain, old-fashioned manual labor. At least, that's what he'd been telling himself for the past hour. Muscles straining, he returned to his task, falling into an easy rhythm of forceful strokes.

''Excuse me.''

It took two more blows before the quietly insistent words sank in. Driving the blade into the tree trunk, he turned. A woman stood nearby, watching him. She carried a bundle of quilts almost as large as she was. He suppressed a smile. Something about her—perhaps her snow-flecked silver-blond hair, or the huge powder-blue eyes, or the triangular, pixieish shape of her face—inspired an irresistible smile. He ruthlessly suppressed it, snagging his flannel shirt from the low-hanging branch of a nearby cedar.

"Can I help you?" he asked, thrusting his arms into the sleeves. "Are you lost?"

She waited, her gaze glittering with some strange emotion. What the hell was she staring at? "My car broke down," she finally said, her voice lightly flavored with the honeyed lilt of the South. He'd heard that accent before and it didn't bring back pleasant images. Was he never to escape the memory of Rhonda?

"I have a phone inside."

Still she waited, her expression revealing an odd combination of hope and resignation. "I'm not from around here," she offered hesitantly. "Maybe you noticed?"

He buttoned his shirt, studying her with an intensity equal to her own. "Yeah, the accent sort of gave you away."

Releasing her breath in a whisper-soft sigh she approached, coming to a halt a scant foot away. "Please—"

Shifting the pile of quilts she held, she fixed her eyes on him. They were startling blue eyes, filled with unicorns and Santa Claus and impossible dreams. He instinctively took a step backward. He didn't deal well with dreamers, not when he remained so steeped in reality. At his actions, the sweet illusions slipped from her eyes, leaving behind a soul-deep weariness. For the first time, he noticed the lavender crescents beneath each lower lid and the pale tautness of flesh over bone marking her exhaustion.

"I meant…" She took an instant to collect herself. *Switching gears,* Alessandro thought. This wasn't the conversation she'd planned to have with him. He couldn't begin to guess how he read her so easily. But there wasn't a doubt in his mind that what she'd intended to say was far different from what he'd now hear. "I was hopin' you'd know who to call. About my car."

Finished with the buttons lining his shirt, he stuffed the tails into his jeans. "There aren't many choices. You passed a small town in the valley before coming up here. They have a garage or two. With a storm moving in, you'll want to get off the mountain as soon as you can."

She closed her eyes for a split second, her lashes dusted with thick wet flakes. They clung for the briefest of moments before melting into diamond droplets. He frowned at the sight. They looked uncomfortably like shimmering tears. Great. A crying elf. Just what he needed for Christmas.

"You're right," she murmured at last. The snow came down harder, coating her and the bundle she carried in pristine white. "There *is* a storm moving in. Best I deal with it sooner rather than later."

"We'd better get inside. Come with me."

He opened the back door and stomped his feet to remove the mud and slush that clung to his boots. She followed his example, her stomping taking the form of a more delicate tapping on the throw rug. It was probably just as well since her shoes wouldn't hold up to a serious pounding. They must be comfortable. He sure couldn't think of any other reason she'd continue to wear hole-laden bits of leather that should have graced a trash can months ago.

He led the way through the kitchen and into a large two-story living area. A fire crackled in the hearth lending a cheerful warmth to the setting. She hesitated just inside the doorway before approaching the fireplace. Carefully, she set her bundle on the floor and crouched protectively next to it, holding her hands out to the flames.

"This is nice," she murmured.

Without the quilts concealing her, he saw that she was slighter than he'd thought. In fact, she looked half-starved. Her denim coat had been repaired so many times, it was a wonder there was enough material left to hold it together. It also appeared to be about three sizes too large, the cuffs falling back to expose delicate wrists and long, capable fingers.

"Your coat doesn't offer much warmth for the sort of weather we're having," he found himself saying. To his surprise, a hint of concern threaded his words.

"North Carolina wasn't this cold when I left. Although I suspect it is by now." She slanted him a quick glance, as if assessing his reaction to the casually offered information. "It took me a while to get here."

His eyes narrowed. "What part of North Carolina?"

"Asheville."

She pronounced it Ash-vul. He thought he'd recognized her accent. This only confirmed it. She came from the same region of the country as his ex-wife, though any similarities ended there. Rhonda had retained the accent while ridding herself of all traces of her mountain heritage. Her tastes ran toward the more sophisticated pleasures, rather than the traditional. He couldn't say the same about the woman before him. He suspected she embodied the traditional, that it was steeped into her very bones.

He frowned, something about her comments rousing the analytical part of his personality. Something about the weather in the mountains.... "I've made the drive from North Carolina before," he offered. "Depending on which route you take and how many hours you're willing to drive each day, you can make it in as few as four days. I'd have thought you'd have seen snow in the mountains by now."

"Not drivin' poor little Babe. I've been on the road for nigh on a month."

"Babe?"

"My car." She flashed him a quick grin. "It seemed appropriate seein' as she's a shade on the pink side."

"Pink."

Her grin widened. It was full and generous and came with an infectious ease that suggested she smiled often, though he had the feeling she hadn't found occasion to smile much recently. It also gave her a mischievous appearance that sat at odds with the nervous tension he sensed lying just beneath the surface.

"Yeah, pink. Cartoon-pig pink, to be exact. I have to confess, it does rouse comment."

"I don't wonder," he muttered. "Your car is in such bad shape it took you a month to get here?"

"Pitiful, isn't it? Though it wasn't just the car." She broke off and turned her head to study the flames crackling cheerfully in the hearth. "There were other considerations."

Financial, he read between the lines. That explained the shoes and threadbare coat. "Worked your way across, did you?"

"It got me here," she acknowledged.

"Here?"

She froze. Slowly her hands dropped to her lap and she snatched a quick, shallow breath. "To California," she managed to say.

He didn't know why he felt the need to press the issue, since it wasn't any of his business. "To this part of California?"

"San Francisco, to be exact."

She responded readily enough, which sat at odds with her tension. He'd half expected her to refuse to answer. People with secrets weren't often this forthcoming, and his little elf was chock-full of secrets. There wasn't a single doubt about that. "This isn't the best route between Asheville and San Francisco. In fact, I'd say this was quite a way off the beaten path."

She bowed her head. "It's where my road led. I just followed."

"Very cryptic." Time to bring an end to this nonsense and get her off his mountain and on her way. "Why don't I find out about arranging for a tow before the weather deteriorates any further. I assume you'll also want to stay at a nearby motel while you're car's being repaired?"

Exhaustion exploded in her face again, along with a painful helplessness. "Yes, please."

"Is something wrong?" he felt compelled to ask. His mouth tightened at the inadvertent question. Apparently the Salvatore code of behavior hadn't been eradicated, even after thirty-five years of hard living. He still had trouble resisting a damsel in distress, despite having learned that women were rarely in true distress and frequently expected more than a simple assist. Maybe that was why he'd been so attracted to Rhonda. For all her flaws, she'd been as independent as they came. Still… He sighed, following the dictates his father, Dom, had done his damnedest to instill from the cradle. "Is there anything I can do to help?"

Her frantic gaze fastened on him, urged him to say something—*do* something. But what she expected of him, he couldn't begin to guess. "Don't you know?" she whispered.

Aw, hell. "I'm a man, sweetheart. You have to tell me what you want." He offered a teasing grin. "Try simple, single-syllable words in short, concise sentences. That tends to work best with me."

She hesitated, her desperation plain to see. Finally, she shook her head, her lashes dipping to conceal the flash of pain that burned in her expression. "No, thanks. The tow truck is enough for now."

For now, huh? Why didn't that surprise him? Without another word, he turned and crossed the room to his study. It only took a minute to place the call and secure a promise that the tow truck would pick up "Babe" within the next two hours. Alessandro checked outside. Taking note of the gathering gloom, he grimaced. It was only one in the afternoon and yet it already looked like sundown. If that truck didn't make an appearance within the next thirty minutes, it wouldn't be coming at all. Already the woman's car was blanketed by a couple inches of brittle, icy snow, not a hint of pink showing through the glaze of white.

He glanced through the study door toward the living room. His guest hadn't moved from her position in front of the fireplace. The reddish glow from the embers licked across her delicate profile, highlighting the small, straight nose, sweeping arch of her cheekbones and gently rounded chin. The paleness of her hair also reflected the firelight, changing the silvery color to a fiery rose. The short cap of silky strands feathered about her head in attractive disarray, making her look more elfin than ever. If it weren't for the small frown drawing her brows together, the aura of Christmas-like enchantment would have been complete. At a guess, her thoughts weren't pleasant ones.

He deliberately turned his back on her before he was tempted to try and take complete charge. Whatever problems plagued her weren't any of his business. Checking the phone book, he placed the second call, determined to find her a place to stay for the night. Unfortunately, the two small motels in town were full, as was the ski lodge perched on the next mountain over. Apparently the promised storm had brought in the skiers and snowboarders from the coast. That didn't leave him many options. If he couldn't get his visitor's car out of his driveway or find a place for her to wait out the storm, she wouldn't be going anyplace anytime soon.

Damn. He rubbed the furrow creasing his forehead. This wasn't how he'd planned to spend the next few days. He craved solitude. Time to think. Time to plan. Time to gather himself for action. Apparently the fates had conspired to make sure he didn't get the time he needed.

Giving in to the inevitable, he crossed the room to join her. For some reason, she drew him, rousing protective instincts that had him crouching beside her in a solicitous manner. "Lou said he'd be here within the next couple hours to pick up your car. So, you might as well take off your coat and make yourself comfortable."

He was close enough to see the rapid give-and-take of her breath and the slight flush that crept across her cheekbones. Was he responsible for that? Perhaps he made her nervous. It wouldn't surprise him. As the tallest and broadest of all the Salvatore boys, he'd long been considered the most intimidating of the lot. And yet, if she found him intimidating, she'd have edged away.

Instead, she swayed closer, the softening of body and gaze betraying an underlying attraction. Was she even aware of her actions? It was as though she felt at ease with him, comfortable in his presence. He'd never had a woman react that way to him in such a short time. He found it had a powerful effect, one he neither anticipated nor wanted. A brief holiday affair wasn't what he'd planned for the next week or so. There were other matters on his mind.

With an economy of motion, he helped her out of her coat and tossed it toward the couch. She wore a man's plaid flannel shirt beneath, the cotton washed into baby-soft pliancy. It clung to her breasts and hips, looking more feminine than he thought it possible for flannel to look.

"So why are you up here all on your lonesome instead of sharin' the holidays with your family?" she asked.

For a moment, he could only stare. How did she know about his family? "Come again?"

She jumped to her feet and plucked a photo from off the mantel, her movements filled with a vitality he suspected to be more characteristic than her earlier stillness. The picture was a recent one showing his beaming father surrounded by Alessandro, his five brothers, their various wives, his six-and-a-half-year-old niece and a healthy smattering of nephews. "This *is* your family, isn't it?"

He relaxed slightly, nodding in acknowledgment. "Good guess."

She stared at the photo with an acute longing almost painful to witness. "If I had a family this impressive, I'd rather spend Christmas with them, not all by my lonesome."

"Who says I won't be spending it with my family?"

"Instinct." She glanced around the comfortable living room and at the personal belongings that had somehow worked their way out of his suitcases and were scattered about. "You look to be dug in for the winter."

"Feminine instinct tells you all that, huh?"

"Well... Maybe a bit more than instinct," she confessed.

More than feminine instinct? He wasn't sure he wanted to know what that might be or what it might indicate. It threatened to build a connection between them he had no intention of encouraging. Even with that decision firmly in mind, he found himself responding. "You're right," he conceded. "This isn't my favorite time of year. I prefer to go through it alone, instead of inflicting myself on my family."

"Now that's a shame."

"They don't mind."

"I'm not so sure. Your poppa appears to be a loving man. I'll bet he isn't too happy about your decision." She smiled down at the portrait. "I'm surprised he hasn't told you as much. I'm guessin' he's the sort who doesn't put up with any nonsense from his sons."

She'd read a lot into a simple photo. The fact that most of what she'd said also happened to be true only made Alessandro all the more wary. "What I choose to do isn't his concern."

She laughed, shooting him a knowing look. "Of course it's his concern. That's what being part of a family is all about."

He preferred not to talk about himself, despite her determination to do just that. "Is that how it is with your family?" he asked. Maybe the question would help turn the tables.

"Once upon a time it was. Not anymore."

"Why not?"

"I only had a sister and she passed on two months ago." She traced each member of the Salvatore clan with a blunt fingernail. "I…I still can't hardly believe she's gone."

Aw, hell! "I'm sorry." He squeezed her shoulder in gentle understanding. Once again, she leaned into his grasp, rather than pulling away from what most would regard as a stranger's touch. A warmth stirred between them that had little to do with the heat blazing from the fireplace. It was a visceral reaction, one he couldn't have governed even if he'd wanted to. Something about her drew him, held him, bound him. He couldn't recall ever having such an intense and instantaneous connection with a woman before. Not even with Rhonda. "You must find this time of the year even more difficult to handle than I do."

She inclined her head, layered strands of silvery-blond fluttering at her temples and across her brow. An image flashed through his mind, an image of his hands thrusting deep into the silken depths at the nape of her neck and feeling the soft caress of her hair rippling through his fingers, teasing the length of his jaw, feathering a tortuous path across his chest. He inhaled sharply and released her. Where the hell had that come from? Dredging up an ounce of common sense, he stepped away from more temptation than he could handle.

She took his abandonment with good grace. ''I guess losing my sister makes me a mite sensitive about family.''

''Understandable.''

She returned the photo to the mantel with notable reluctance. Staring at the Salvatore clan for another moment, she set her chin at a determined angle and swiveled to face him. ''Now, don't let my sad news get you down,'' she ordered briskly. ''That wasn't my intent. I just wanted to point out that family isn't something you should take for granted. That's all.''

''As I said… They understand.''

She gave a decisive nod. ''I don't doubt it for a minute. All the more reason to turn to them in your time of need.''

''My time of need?'' Presumptuous little sprite. He was determined to bring her up short. ''You may consider yourself qualified to lecture me about family, but I suggest you mind your own business. At a guess, you have more than your fair share of problems to deal with right now without worrying about mine.''

She brushed the verbal slap aside as though it were no more than a gentle reprimand. ''And I'll be dealin' with them soon enough. But you're a man with a family the size of a couple of football teams,'' she persisted. ''A man, moreover, who chooses to be all on his own at Christmas. That means you're needy. And when a body's needy there's no better help than one's family. Mark my words. If they knew you were heartsick, they'd be up here in a flash, every last one of them.''

Fury ripped through him. ''First off, I'm *not* heartsick. Nor am I needy. What I am is a man who wants you to get the hell—''

She'd fixed those light blue eyes on him again and he found the words jamming in his throat before they could be spoken. He swore beneath his breath, using a flavorful range of Italian expletives. For some reason—maybe because they were the first he'd learned as an impressionable ten-year-old—they came more easily to mind. He gritted his teeth. The motels were full, he reminded himself. The weather was doing its level best to work itself into a full-fledged blizzard. And the woman blinking innocently up at him would be stuck as his guest for at least a day, if not two or three.

''What I am is a man in desperate need of a cup of coffee.'' His voice had assumed the Italian undertones it often acquired whenever he found himself in stressful situations. He could only hope she didn't hear it, or if she did, didn't understand the significance as clearly as his brothers would have. ''Would you like one while you wait?''

If she guessed what he'd originally planned to say, she didn't let on. ''I'd appreciate that.'' She swiped her hands across the seat of her jeans with an energetic slap. ''Would you like me to fix it for you?''

''Now why would I want that?''

The softness of his voice gave her pause, but she shrugged it off with a smile. ''Call it Southern hospitality.''

''My home, my hospitality. I'll take care of it.''

"Sure you don't need my help?"

There was something odd about this entire situation. Something about *her* that felt out of kilter. Nothing about her—from the abruptness of her arrival, to her strange reaction to him, to her meddlesome questions—made a bit of sense. Maybe once he'd reignited his brain cells with some caffeine he'd figure it out. Or better still, maybe he'd ask a few of the questions he should have when she'd first turned up on his doorstep.

"Why don't you enjoy the fire while I fix us both a cup," he suggested. "How do you take it?"

Her smile faded at his question, the vitality seeping from her. Now what had he said to prompt that reaction? She crossed to the couch and curled up at one end. "It's a reasonable question," she murmured, more to herself than to him. "I take it white, thank you kindly. And having something of a sweet tooth, I wouldn't object if you tossed in a lump or two of sugar."

"Coming right up."

It didn't take long for him to brew a fresh pot of coffee. He used the opportunity to compose a long list of questions. Topping the list would be her name. He couldn't believe they hadn't introduced themselves. So much for hospitality, Southern or otherwise. Filling two oversize mugs with a helping of the extra-strong brew, he returned to the living room.

"Here you go, Miss...?"

He stood at the end of the couch, holding the two mugs of steaming hot coffee and frowned in disbelief. His visitor had fallen sound asleep. Incredible. This had to be the most bizarre day he'd experienced in a long time. He set the mugs on the coffee table and took a seat in a large wing chair near the fire. Dropping his feet on the ottoman, he stared broodingly at the woman.

What on earth was he to do with her? Even if Lou came for her car, there wasn't anyplace for her to spend the night other than here. He glanced at the pile of quilts she'd deposited so carefully on his floor. She couldn't have driven clear across the country with nothing more than the clothes on her back and a bunch of handmade quilts. He supposed he should check to see if she had any luggage in Babe's trunk and bring it in. Once he had her unloaded, the matter of where she'd spend the night would be resolved and out of her hands by the time she awoke. No discussion, no argument. Then he could ask a few of those questions nagging at him.

As though in response to his intense regard, the quilts on the floor shifted. Before Alessandro could do more than bolt upright in his chair, a child dug out from under the colorful mountain. He sat for a moment, staring at the unfamiliar surroundings.

"What the...?"

At the sound of Alessandro's voice, the child's inky-dark gaze fastened briefly on him before shifting to the woman. Instantly, he broke into a wide grin that revealed eight serrated nubs, four teeth centered on the bottom and four on top. He didn't call for his mother the way Alessandro's niece and nephews had often done in similar circumstances, but crawled free of his temporary bed. Unsteadily gaining his feet, he made a determined beeline for his mother.

Alessandro caught the boy before he reached his goal. If ever a woman needed her sleep, this one did. He half expected a tearful response. But the boy didn't utter a sound. With an expression of utter trust, he allowed Alessandro to return to the chair and promptly made himself comfortable by curling up against the broad chest supporting him and pointing his diapered bottom skyward. Popping a thumb in his mouth, the boy closed his eyes and returned to sleep.

Alessandro released his breath in a half laugh, half groan. Definitely an interesting day. Who'd have thought the elf had come toting a baby. No wonder she'd looked so exhausted. Working her way across country with an infant in tow couldn't have been simple or easy. Aware that he'd be stuck in the chair for a while, he stretched out a hand toward his coffee mug. Unfortunately, he couldn't reach it without getting up. He didn't dare risk that.

Damn.

Shifting to a more comfortable position, he surrendered. Some things simply couldn't be controlled. And those that couldn't, he'd learned to endure. Time to start enduring. The boy's small body generated a surprising amount of heat and Alessandro closed his eyes, sinking deeper into the leather chair cushions. Between the physical exertion of the morning and far too many sleepless nights due to his dreams of Rhonda, catching a little shut-eye struck him as an excellent idea.

A pervasive baby-scented warmth seeped into Alessandro's bones. He liked the smell. It reminded him of… Of family. A slight smile relaxed the hard curves of his mouth and he tucked his bundle more securely beneath his chin. The dark silken hair caressed his jaw and a tiny heartbeat fluttered close to his own, vulnerable, yet determined. It was a reassuring sensation, an expression of new life.

His smile faded. Now he knew he must be exhausted. He was getting downright sappy. Babies weren't adorable or reassuring. They were damp, noisy and they belonged in someone else's arms. He'd tolerate this one for now. But as soon as the elf awoke, he'd dump the kid on her and keep a safe distance until they both left. That decided, Alessandro drifted off.

Sleep came immediately—a more peaceful sleep than he'd experienced in months.

CHAPTER TWO

Still seven days before Christmas…

SHE *came to him again, all silk and sweetness and
heady feminine perfume. Her hazel eyes were alight
with laughter, laughter echoed in the eager, honeyed
tones of her voice. Her enthusiasm knew no bounds—
whether it was for a soft purple crocus pushing
through its cap of snow, or for the spread of gourmet
food he'd picked up in town, or simply for his touch.
Everything brought her joy. And she returned that joy
with her every act and deed.*

*She ate with gusto, spoke with vibrant enthusiasm,
made love with unstinting generosity. He could see
her more clearly now than in his previous dreams.
She stood in a shaft of moonlight, caped in a satin
cloak of pale strawberry hair, her nudity silvered with
moonlight. She held out her arms in welcome, calling
to him with her siren's song.*

*He was helpless to resist. He wanted her. Needed
her.*

Took her.

"Alessandro…? Nick? Nicky! Where are you?"

The woman's cry startled Alessandro and the boy
he held. Reacting with impressive speed, he recovered
his balance before they both toppled to the floor.
"Easy," he reassured the woman, his words sleep

25

roughened. He climbed from the chair and approached. "I have him over here."

She stood in front of the scattered quilts, trembling. "I'm sorry." She thrust a hand through her hair and tousling the short, silky strands into further disorder. "It's gotten so dark, I didn't see you. I just saw... Saw..."

"Saw the empty blankets and thought—Nicky, is it?"

"Nick. I should call him Nick. Nicky's a baby's name and he's not..." He heard the tears in her voice, heard, too, the quick, shallow give-and-take of her breath. "He's not much of a baby anymore."

Something about the intensity of her turmoil urged him to drag her into his arms and comfort her in all the ways a man best comforted a woman. No doubt it had something to do with her fear or perhaps the pervasive femininity that cloaked her. It drew him as nothing else could. But that option wasn't available to him. So instead, he pitched his voice to soothe. "You saw the empty blankets and thought Nick had wandered off."

"Yes. It scared me."

Alessandro set the boy on the floor. With a gleeful cry, he toddled to the woman, flinging himself against her legs. She applauded his efforts with an uneven laugh and swung him into her arms, hugging him tight. He returned the hug with enthusiasm, bursting into an incomprehensible stream of baby babble. Alessandro suppressed a grin. For such a little guy, he had a ridiculously deep voice, the sound not much more than a gruff rumble. Even though there wasn't a single recognizable word, the woman gave Nick her full attention until he finally ran dry. Finished relaying his information, he aimed a wet kiss at her mouth and then squirmed in her arms for release.

She obediently put him down before glancing at Alessandro. He found the wealth of unsuppressed emotion almost painful to observe. ''Thank you for watching him.''

He shrugged, doing his best to ease her distress with an air of calm. He'd often found it worked best with his own family. They all had the regrettable tendency to respond with fiery passion to every situation, regardless of whether the development was a crisis or cause for celebration. He'd learned as a child that being the rock in the midst of the storm helped anchor everyone else. As he grew, his height and breadth only added to the image of strength and control.

''I don't know how much watching I did,'' he said. ''Apparently Nick decided he hadn't gotten enough sleep the first time 'round. So I offered to join him when he settled down for a second nap.''

''I didn't hear him wake. I don't understand it.'' She dropped to her knees, folding the handmade quilts with swift, jerky movements at odds with her earlier gracefulness. ''I kept him close so I'd hear.''

''You were sound asleep when I came back with the coffee. I decided not to disturb you when he woke, and fortunately, Nick proved cooperative.'' Alessandro flipped on the overhead lights, driving the dusky shadows from the darkened room, and crossed to revive the dying fire. ''You looked like you needed your sleep.''

She confirmed his guess with an abrupt nod. ''I was on the road most of the night.''

Removing the fireplace screen, he tossed a couple of logs onto the grate. ''Why was that?''

She started to answer, hesitating at the last minute. He suspected she'd rather not explain, but after a moment's consideration, she shrugged. "You might as well know the truth." Digging in her pocket she pulled a wad of crumpled bills and a handful of change. She set it on the table next to the two mugs of cold coffee, smoothing each bill with great precision. "That's every last penny I have to my name."

Alessandro winced. Replacing the fire screen, he rocked back on his heels and did a swift, silent count. Not good. At most she had a whole twenty-five bucks heaped there. "Kind of tough to get a car repaired with that. Not to mention putting a roof over your head and food on your table."

Nick toddled over to examine the money and she scooped it up, returning it to her pocket. "I'm not afraid of hard work. I suspect I can clean rooms in exchange for a place to stay."

"Not likely." No doubt that was one of the ways she'd worked her way from North Carolina to California. Too bad it wouldn't work here. Giving himself time to think, he crossed to a closet on the far side of the room and opened the door. Spying the box he wanted, he dragged it out and presented it to Nick. The boy took one look at the overflowing carton of toys and crowed in delight. "Have at it, kid. My treat."

The woman laughed in amazement. "Goodness gracious! That's more toys than he's seen in all his born days. Come to think of it, it's more toys than *I've* ever seen."

Alessandro grinned. "You saw my family photo. With all those kids, we keep the cabin well-supplied with playthings. I think the general consensus was better safe than sorry.''

''It must make a nice treat for them. I'll bet they love coming here. Though your idea of a cabin and mine are somewhat different. Where I come from a cabin is a whole lot smaller and rougher. No more than a one or two room affair.'' Her gaze swept the cypress-trimmed cathedral ceiling. ''Not a mansion like this.''

''True. But cabin sounds so much more modest.''

Her mouth curved into a quick smile which faded to an apprehensive frown. He could tell she'd just absorbed his earlier comment about the local motels. ''You said…not likely. Why isn't it likely that I can clean rooms in exchange for a place to stay?''

''The motels in the area are booked solid between now and the New Year.''

She stilled. ''You neglected to mention that earlier.''

''I thought I'd save the news until the tow truck showed up.'' He crossed to the window and glanced outside. The storm hadn't lessened any. Rather it had grown worse. A white lump remained in the middle of the driveway, its blanket of icy snow far thicker than it had been earlier. It didn't come as any surprise to find Babe hadn't been moved. ''Though I doubt that tow's going to happen. This storm hit harder than anyone anticipated.''

''When do you think he'll come?''

''No time soon.'' Alessandro threw her a warning look over his shoulder. ''Not that you have enough in your pocket for a tow, let alone car repairs, even if Lou does put in an appearance.''

To his amazement, she smiled confidently. ''I'll

work something out with the mechanic. I'll bet I can pick up a waitressing job. I'm experienced at that. And if the motels are as busy as you say, they're bound to need a part-timer to lend a hand.'' She practically vibrated with cheerful optimism. Quite a switch from her earlier distress. Based on what he'd observed so far, he suspected her current attitude came closer to reflecting her true personality. ''Maybe someone will be kind enough to take in a boarder. A widow lady or a pensioner. They always appreciate extra pocket money.''

He deliberately wiped all inflection from his voice. ''Could be.'' Though he doubted it. There were usually a slew of college students only too eager to earn a few bucks over the holidays, especially if it meant they could ski during their off-hours. ''You still haven't explained what you're doing here.''

''Time enough to deal with that later,'' she retorted briskly. ''I think the first order of business is to figure out where Nick and I are going to stay for the night.''

''There isn't any choice. You'll have to stay here.''

''Look, Alessandro, before you make offers you might not want to keep, there's something I need to—'' She broke off, her expression switching from determined to appalled.

He stiffened. *Alessandro*. She'd called him Alessandro. ''How the hell do you know my name?'' he questioned with biting softness. Now that he thought about it, this was the second time she'd used it. She'd called to him when she'd first awoken, before panicking about Nick. If he hadn't been jerked out of a sound sleep, he'd have caught her error sooner. ''We never introduced ourselves.''

''I can explain—''

"Have we met?" He approached, crowding her against the sofa. The quilts tumbled from her arms to the floor again, cascading to her feet in a stream of vibrant color. "Or is this some sort of setup? *Who the hell are you?*"

She stared at him, unicorns and Santa Claus and impossible dreams returning to her eyes. He halted abruptly, unwilling to invade further into such alien territory. "Don't you remember me?" she pleaded.

"Should I?"

"I was hopin' you might. We met a while back."

He swept her with a swift, penetrating glance, struggling to find something even remotely familiar about her. From what he could see of her beneath the ill-fitting clothing, there was lean strength in the fine-boned frame and an appealing delicacy to her features. She met his gaze unflinchingly, her expression open and straightforward, if a shade wary. Not even the unusual blue shade of her eyes struck a chord, though the stoic resolve reflected there gave him pause. No. He'd have remembered if they'd ever met.

"It must have been a while back," he said, giving her the benefit of the doubt. "Are you related to my ex-wife? Did we meet at the wedding?"

Her jaw clenched. "No. We met two years ago this coming March."

March? She'd chosen an interesting time period, one with a big, black hole right in the middle of it. His mouth tightened. Or did she already know that? After all, the events of that month weren't a secret. He analyzed her expression, searching for some clue to what she had planned. Something wasn't right about this—about *her*. He'd suspected it from the start. If he hadn't been so distracted by his reaction to her, he'd have pursued that sense of wrongness sooner. Whatever the case, he'd had enough.

He moved away, giving them both some much-needed breathing space. They might never have met before—at least, that he could remember—but that didn't mean he wouldn't have been interested in getting to know her more intimately, if circumstances had been different. He was forced to acknowledge the underlying attraction, an irrational, if undeniable firing of the senses. Still… Common sense urged caution—and he'd learned through years of rocky experience to listen to his common sense.

"Okay, fine. Let's say I believe your claim that we've met before. You just happened to be driving by when your car broke down?" he questioned skeptically. "Your arrival here is sheer coincidence?"

She lifted her chin, inherent pride implicit in every line of her body. "No, it's not coincidence. I knew you'd be here and came to find you."

Alessandro folded his arms across his chest. "How did you guess where I'd be? The cabin belongs to my entire family."

"Your brother, Luc, gave me directions. I visited your family business—Salvatores—before coming."

This tale was getting worse by the minute. "You knew enough about me to track me down in San Francisco? At work, no less?"

"Yes."

"And Luc, after only one meeting, told you where to find me?" He fired the question at her. "Or have you met him before, too."

"Yes! No." She thrust her hands into her hair and shoved the flyaway bangs out of her face. Taking a deep breath, she fought for control. "No, I'd never met Luc or any of your family before showin' up on their doorstep. And yes, Luc gave me directions after just one meeting.''

''And why would he do that?''

''So I could give you—'' Her voice broke, but she made a swift recovery. ''So I could give you something.''

''What?''

Her hands closed into fists and her mouth worked for an instant before she managed to get the words out. ''I came to give you Nick. He's...'' A sheen of tears glistened in her eyes. ''He's your son.''

Fury poured through him in waves. ''Who the hell are you and what sort of sick joke is this?'' He kept his voice low, but it still bit. She flinched, though she didn't back down.

''It's not a joke.''

''Are you trying to tell me that you and I were lovers?'' His laugh held a harsh edge. ''Pull the other one, sweetheart. There isn't a chance that once I'd had you in my bed I'd forget such a memorable occasion.''

Her gaze fastened on him for an endless moment and he felt as if she were searching for something deep within him, fighting to elicit a response. Whatever she wanted, he didn't possess. Rhonda had exorcised most of the gentler human qualities from him long ago. The silence stretched between them, drawn taut with unmistakable tension. It wasn't quite a battle of wills, but it definitely resonated with the sort of emotional turbulence that had existed between men and women since the beginning of time.

At long last, her lashes flickered downward, cutting off her thoughts. No doubt she was considering her options. Not that she had any. He had no intention of having her responsibilities dumped on him. If she hadn't already figured that out, he'd make it crystal clear in the next couple of minutes.

''Are you ready to tell me the truth?'' he demanded. ''Are you doing this in the hopes of getting money from me? Or are you just tired of taking care of your kid and looking for a convenient place to abandon him?''

She didn't react with the indignant anger his words should have roused. To his amazement, compassion crept into her gaze, a compassion he neither wanted nor needed. ''You sound so cynical.''

''I'm feeling rather cynical right now.''

''Nick's your son, Alessandro. A simple blood test will prove it.''

''When and where was he conceived?'' His mouth twisted. ''And perhaps I should ask…with whom?''

She stiffened, his words clearly firing her resolve. Her mouth firmed and her posture straightened to painful erectness. Determination ignited the vividness of her eyes, eclipsing the earlier compassion, and she faced him with a ferocity at direct odds with her fey appearance. ''It was two years ago next March. In fact, Nick was conceived on the first day of spring in a pretty little cabin on the outskirts of Asheville, North Carolina. A *real* cabin, rustic and simple and hewn from the surrounding trees with loving hands and hearts. He'll be a year old on Christmas Day. His mother's name is Meg. Meg Williams. Ring any bells, Mr. Salvatore?''

Meg. He tried out the name, finding it had a disturbing familiarity, though he could have sworn he'd never met anyone by that name. "I was in Asheville that March."

"So you admit it?"

"No way, sweetheart. I'm not admitting anything."

"You accuse me of trying to escape my responsibilities. What about you?" Despair drove the sweet illusions from her eyes. "Are you going to stand there and deny your part in Nick's existence? I wouldn't have thought so poorly of you, Alessandro. You always struck me as the upstanding sort."

"Are you saying we had a one-night stand while I was there?" he forced himself to ask. He didn't want to concede even that much. Unfortunately, he wasn't in any position to defend his innocence.

"I'm not saying any such thing. I'm flat-out telling you it happened. And it wasn't a one-night stand. You had a two-week relationship with Nick's momma, Meg. You also claimed to love her." A spark of indignation surged through her voice, pain underscoring every word. "Are those sorts of affairs so common, you don't even remember? Or was it the woman you were with who proved forgettable?"

He wasn't ready to tell her about his days in Asheville. He needed time to analyze her angle before revealing any chinks in his armor. "They're not common. Which is all the more reason why I'd remember fathering a child, particularly if the relationship was as serious as you're suggesting." There was another factor insuring that Nick couldn't be his. "I'm also scrupulous about practicing safe sex. I don't consider it a woman's sole responsibility and never have."

"Nor do you trust women enough to allow them to take the responsibility."

Her words had a flat finality that stopped him cold. "How do you know that?"

"Your youngest brother, Pietro, made that mistake. Your niece, Toni, is the result. And even though Pietro married Toni's momma and their marriage has been a lovin' one, you were determined not to allow a similar accident to happen to you. At least, that's what you told Meg." Her mouth curved into a bitter-sweet smile. "I guess you could say fate has a flair for the ironic."

Once again he felt a disturbing familiarity with the name. "Is that you? You're Meg?"

She hesitated for so long, he didn't think she'd answer. "I'm Lauren Williams," she eventually said, her voice rife with a bone-deep exhaustion. "Meg is...*was* my sister."

"Was?"

Lauren's obvious distress aroused another surge of the protective instinct he'd experienced earlier. What was it about her that cut through the defenses he'd built over the years? Her waiflike appearance? His appreciation for the inherent strength that underscored her every word and action? Or was it simply a gut-level attraction to her as a woman?

"My sister died a few months ago, remember? I mentioned it earlier."

"Right. I'm sorry." He didn't want to push when she was so obviously upset, but he didn't have any choice. "I assume she's the one who told you I'm Nick's father."

"Yes."

"Is there any possibility she's mistaken?" He couldn't think of a more tactful way to phrase the question.

She acknowledged the effort with a slight smile. "None."

Alessandro frowned as another thought occurred to him. "You said *we'd* met. When was that?"

"My sister and I were together that first day. You and Meg hit it off from the start."

"Where was this?"

"At a small restaurant tucked in the foothills outside of Asheville. A place called LuLu's."

He shook his head in frustration. "I'm sorry. I don't remember. Do you have any way at all of substantiating your claim?"

She paused again and he knew without a doubt that she was keeping something from him. She'd hesitated like that once before, but he couldn't remember what question he'd asked at the time. He'd make damned sure he paid attention from here on out.

"The blood test will substantiate my claim. You don't need more than that."

Need or deserve? Alessandro couldn't help but wonder. He thrust a hand through his hair and paced toward the hearth. The fire licked hungrily at the logs he'd added. The ruby embers beneath the grate hissed, relieved by an occasional pop and the accompanying shower of sparks. Lauren acted so certain, he had the nasty suspicion she might be telling the truth—at least, the truth as she knew it. He glanced uneasily at the boy who was sitting on the floor by the carton of toys, examining each and every one of them with an intentness surprising in one so young. Could Nick actually be his? Could he have a son?

He dismissed the possibility with a quick shake of his head. No. No way. For one thing, he didn't go in for one-night stands—or even two-week stands. And for another, Lauren was right. He didn't take foolish chances or trust his partner to handle something as vital as birth control. If he'd been with this Meg, he'd have taken precautions. Children weren't in the foreseeable future—at least, not in his foreseeable future.

He swung around to face Lauren. "So what now?"

"I'm hopin' you'll want to get to know your son." She smiled at the boy with a tenderness that transfigured her. With that simple curve of her lips she went from elf to angel. "A boy should be close to his father."

"And if the test proves I'm not Nick's father?"

She didn't appear concerned by the possibility. "That's not going to happen. Even if you don't believe me, look at him. He's the image of you."

He lifted an eyebrow. "He looks like a typical baby. In case you haven't noticed, I don't bear any resemblance to a baby whatsoever."

The corners of her mouth trembled into another smile and a soft, silvery laugh escaped. "No, you don't. I was referring to the shape of his face and color of his hair and eyes. They're the same pitch-black as yours."

"I'm not the only man in the world with dark eyes."

She sighed. "True. That's why I'm suggesting a paternity test. That way you'll know for certain."

"I'll need to make some calls to find out where we can have the procedure done."

"If it's too far away, it'll have to wait," she informed him. "I still need to have someone fix my car. And to be honest, I'm exhausted."

She looked it, too. Not that he'd allow sympathy to interfere with his handling of the situation.

Something didn't add up and until he found out what, he refused to trust anything she said. ''I gather that means your car really did break down? It wasn't just an excuse?''

''It pulled into your driveway on a hope and a prayer. It won't be going anywhere anytime soon.''

''Convenient.''

He'd succeeded in angering her. Just as well. Having her angry would make it easier for him to maintain an emotional distance. After all, he'd had years of experience being the calm in the midst of unending storms of passion. If there were two qualities Salvatores were renowned for, it was passion and charm, qualities that had both managed to pass him by. He'd found that the more worked up those around him became, the calmer his own reactions. If Lauren chose to respond like a Salvatore, it would make his job all the easier.

''As far as I'm concerned, it's not the least bit convenient,'' she retorted. ''I can't even drive myself to the store for food or diapers.''

''In that case, I hope you have enough to last the next couple of days.''

''Why?''

''Because neither of us are leaving here anytime soon.''

She darted to the window and stared out, her dismay obvious. ''I can't even see my car.''

''If I were a suspicious man, I'd say your timing was opportune.''

''You are a suspicious man and my timing was lousy,'' she informed him absently.

She knew he was a suspicious man? An ungovernable annoyance flashed through him and he released his breath in a silent sigh. So much for being the dispassionate Salvatore. "If you intend to keep up the pretense that we've met before, it's going to be a long couple of days."

"Pretense?" Lauren turned to face him. She was framed by the window and backlit by a tempest of snow swirling on savage eddies of wind. He had trouble reading her expression, but not the indignation of her tone. "It's not a pretense."

"So you've said. Time will tell." He inclined his head in the direction of the kitchen. "Come on. I missed out on a cup of coffee earlier. I suspect we could both use a cup now."

"First I'd like to unload the car. It's been a while since I last changed Nick." At the sound of his name, the boy glanced up from the toys spread around him and beamed. She returned his grin with one of her own. Alessandro couldn't help but notice the unmistakable resemblance between them. They both shared the same wide, generous mouth that slid into a smile with a natural ease he envied. "He's also going to be hungry for a snack soon."

"Any snacks you left in the car will be frozen by now. You'll have to see if I have anything that will do."

"In that case, let's hope you have yogurt with fruit in it. Nick likes it mixed in with just about everything he eats."

"Everything? You're kidding."

"'Fraid not." She ticked off on her fingers. "He eats peach yogurt with his applesauce. Raspberry yogurt with peas. Strawberry-banana yogurt with chicken. As long as there's yogurt mixed in with his meal, down it goes, slick as pig grease."

"Yogurt and chicken? That's disgusting."

"Not according to your son."

Damn. It only took a brief two-minute conversation for her to slip beneath his defenses and bewitch him into relaxing his guard. How the hell had she pulled that off? No one had ever managed it in such a short time. Not even Rhonda. "Don't call him that."

"What? Your son?" Her jaw jutted out at a defiant angle. "Facts are facts, Alessandro. That's who Nick is. Protesting the truth isn't going to change it any."

"His paternity hasn't been established to my satisfaction."

"Maybe not, but the test will take care of that minor detail. Meanwhile, I suggest you start getting used to the idea."

"Wrong. What we're going to do is take this situation one step at a time. No games. No assumptions. And no great leaps of faith. Until I have positive proof in hand, we keep this as impersonal as possible."

She stared at him in stunned disbelief. Then the corners of her eyes crinkled and her mouth tilted into a broad, quivering grin. "Oh, Alessandro. I should have known. Any other Salvatore would have taken one look at Nicky and allowed emotion to take over."

"I'm not like the others."

"True. But you'd begun to change. You were learning. The weeks you spent with Meg opened you up. It was quite amazing to watch. Maybe if you'd stayed longer in North Carolina, the changes would have taken." She caught her lip between her teeth. "Maybe Meg would have made more of an impact."

"Don't count on it."

She held up her hands in casual surrender, though he could tell his words had impacted harder than he'd intended. He'd have to be more cautious in the future. There was a difference between disengaging his emotions and acting like a coldhearted bastard. "All right, fine. If you'd rather keep your distance from your—" She broke off with a rueful shrug. "From Nick? Feel free. He's young enough that it won't do him any lasting harm, especially so long as I'm here to give him as much love and attention as he could want. The one you'll be hurtin' most is yourself."

"Another of your Southern homilies?" No doubt they were as much a part of her as her pride and the mountain spirit that imbued her with its essence. "Just what I need. A pint-size sprite without funds or a roof over her head landing on my doorstep and taking it upon herself to lecture me about my familial obligations and emotional welfare."

"Oh, I don't think the South has exclusive claim on that particular homily." She poked her index finger in his direction. "And I may be a pint-size woman without kith or kin, other than Nick, but at least I have my priorities straight—family first, last and in between. And at least I'm not hiding here when I should be with my relatives. Nor am I withholding my emotions from an innocent child."

"A child who might not be my son."

Her eyes flashed from a soft, powder-blue to an electric color that blazed with incandescent heat. "Why should that even matter? Do you only parcel out your affection to those you deem worthy? It can't possibly be because you're not sure whether or not he's true family. Family doesn't matter to you all that much, or you'd be with them, especially at this time of year."

An unaccustomed anger ripped through him. "Drop it, Lauren. It's none of your business."

"It is when it affects Nick. He deserves better than what you have to offer." Her voice softened and she held out a hand in appeal. "Where's your heart, Alessandro? What happened to the man I knew in North Carolina? How could you have forgotten your weeks there? It meant something to you. I know it did."

He refused to explain, refused to believe the man she described even existed. "Assuming you're telling me the truth, that Alessandro is lost. He has been for a long time."

She flinched from his words, rejecting them with a quick, adamant shake of her head. "I can't accept that."

"You're going to have to."

She fought an internal battle, one he'd have given a hefty share of his bank balance to have listened in on. Was she going to call an end to this game? Or was she trying to determine her next line of attack? Once she realized emotional blackmail didn't work, perhaps she'd employ logic. Or maybe she'd wrap her arms around him and slip her wide, generous mouth over his. He closed his eyes. Oh, man. He definitely needed that coffee.

Finally, she gave a brisk nod. "I guess that's that. If you can't—or won't—remember, I have no choice."

He'd regret asking this next question, but he asked anyway. "No choice about what?"

"I'm gonna find what you lost. I'm going to dig around until I uncover that other Alessandro."

Aw, hell. "No, Lauren. You're not."

"Oh, it's not for your sake." Determination settled over her. "Nick needs a daddy who can love him. He deserves to have the man I met in North Carolina. And I'm not leaving here until that's what he gets."

CHAPTER THREE

Six days before Christmas...

SHE *came to him again, all silk and sweetness and heady feminine perfume. They were outside in the snow, playing in the drifts like children. He could hear his own laughter, deep and clear, ringing through the crisp mountain air. She'd done that for him, he realized in amazement. She'd returned to him the joy of laughter. It had been a long time since he'd taken pleasure in the sheer simplicity of such a fundamental act.*

She peeked at him from behind the trunk of an ancient oak, its mighty limbs bearing the hint of new-born leaves through the dusting of winter's last snow. She called to him. And finally, finally, *he could hear her lilting voice. It joined them on some level, resonated straight through to the core of him, softening the hardness within and connecting with the most elemental part of his spirit. It was the voice of the mountains, rolling and proud and solid, and silvered with a generous helping of humor.*

"Time's a'wastin', boy. Catch me if you can."

"Who are you calling boy?" he demanded, charging after her.

Her bright laughter snagged at a place that had once held his heart, filling it, expanding it, inflaming it. The chase didn't last long. He captured her in his arms and they tumbled into a bed of powder-soft snow. Her long, cornsilk hair spread around her in a halo of rosy-gold, framing Rhonda's bold, handsome features and distinctive hazel eyes.

"Home is where your heart is, darlin'," she whispered. "Where do you keep your heart?"

"You'll always have it."

"Promise?"

"Promise."

"And you'll always have mine."

She lifted her mouth to his and he was helpless to resist. He wanted her. Needed her.

Took her.

Alessandro awoke with a start, the fragments of his dream clinging with relentless determination. He groaned. Rhonda *again*. It defied understanding—not just because he continued to dream about a woman he hadn't loved in years, but also because the events in his dreams had never happened. It took a full minute to separate fantasy from reality and realize what had disturbed his sleep.

Lauren was up again, moving cautiously around the bedroom she shared with Nick. It had to be at least the third time tonight. Did year-old children wake so often? He knew from tales his brothers had told that newborns didn't allow their parents a lot of sleep, but hadn't known it continued for so many months. Her footsteps padded to the general location of the crib he'd dragged down from the attic. Then she slipped into the hallway and tiptoed to the living area and on toward the kitchen. At the sound of the outside door opening and closing, he tossed aside the covers and escaped his bed.

This couldn't be good.

A shadow of movement drifted along the side of the house past his bay window and Alessandro deliberately left his bedroom in darkness until he could determine her purpose. Moving to a more advantageous line of sight near the window seat, he saw Lauren standing not far from the protection of the overhanging eaves, staring out at the woods. The snowstorm had abated for the moment and a fitful moon peered through the heavy clouds, its light enveloping her.

She looked small and delicate in comparison to her surroundings. Alessandro thrust a hand through his hair, frowning. Her coat couldn't offer much protection, anymore than the bits of moth-eaten leather sewn together in a poor imitation of a pair of shoes. If she didn't come back in soon, he'd go out and insist she utilize an ounce of common sense. If she got sick, he'd have her to care for, as well as Nick. And even though he baby-sat his nephews on rare occasions and had a rudimentary knowledge of which end to feed and which to change, there'd usually been someone more experienced around to deal with all those nasty baby details.

"Cut the crap, Salvatore," Alessandro muttered beneath his breath. "Having to take care of her and the kid isn't what has you all worked up. Admit it."

He was worried about her.

As though conceding his point about her vulnerability, Lauren wrapped her arms around her waist and lowered her head in the face of the bitter ferocity of the wind. Reaching for the chain around his neck, Alessandro swore softly. When would he remember that it wasn't there anymore and that it never would be again? And when would he stop giving in to what could only be an emotional crutch? With a piercing shriek, the snowstorm resumed, spitting an endless barrage of icy shards earthward. And in the last twinkling of moonlight, before the clouds obscured it, he realized that Lauren's shoulders were quivering.

Dammit all! She was crying.

He didn't wait any longer. Yanking on a pair of jeans and snatching up a shirt, he raced from the room. He couldn't say why he felt such an overwhelming urgency. He only knew he had to get to Lauren and reassure her that they'd work everything out over the coming weeks. Thrusting his arms into his shirt sleeves, he didn't bother with the buttons, but charged barefoot from the warmth of the house, pelting flat-out through the icy snow to her side. He didn't waste time on discussion, but snatched her slight figure into the safety of his arms.

She didn't shriek in surprise or struggle against his hold, as he'd expected. Instead, she yielded, curling into him and wrapping her arms around his neck, a tiny hiccuping sob confirming his worst fears. She *was* crying. His response came without hesitation, arising from an instinct he'd have sworn he didn't possess. He enfolded her in a tighter embrace and whispered a gentle reassurance into her damp, silky hair.

She felt warm and soft and disturbingly feminine in his arms. He'd expected more angles than curves. But what he found was a ripeness of form, both sleek and womanly. Her unfettered breasts flattened against his bare chest, her shirt and jacket providing far too little coverage for his peace of mind. It would seem he wasn't the only one to have thrown on whatever clothes came to hand before bolting from the house.

"Don't cry, Lauren." He fought to keep all trace of an Italian accent from his voice. It was too great a betrayal. "Everything will work out, you'll see."

"How did you know I was crying?" She buried her face in his shoulder. "I snuck outside so you wouldn't hear."

His mouth tugged upward. "Call it a wild stab in the dark."

"Not so wild," she muttered.

"Okay, not so wild." He tromped toward the back door, the snow biting his toes into numbness. Apparently gallantry didn't come without a price—not that there was a chance in hell he'd have delayed getting to her while he wasted time shoving his feet into boots or grabbing a jacket. "The real question is *why* you're crying."

"Nothing. Everything."

"That explains it." This was his fault. He'd been too hard on her. He didn't have to deny fathering Nick right off the bat. He could have waited and let the lab results do the dirty work for him. "Listen… If you're worried about finances, Salvatores is always on the lookout for dedicated employees. We even have onsite child-care facilities. You can have Nick close by while we figure out who and where his father might be."

Her head jerked upward and she banged his shoulder with her fist. "You're his father, you idiot. And I've already found you."

He grimaced. So much for letting the test results do the dirty work for him. One of these days he might learn to keep his mouth shut. "Time will tell," he limited himself to saying. Entering the house through the back door, he released her. She paced in the direction of the kitchen while he stood on the throw rug just inside the house and wiped off the rapidly melting snow.

Turning to face him, her breath caught in a gasp. "You're barefoot!" she exclaimed. "Have you lost your ever-lovin' mind?"

"Me?" He snorted in disbelief. "Honey, I'm not the one outside in the middle of a snowstorm, in tears."

"I was thinking." She assumed a defensive posture, her chin set at a stubborn angle, her spine ruler-straight. "I have my best thoughts when I'm outside."

"Your best thoughts come in the middle of a blizzard while you're crying your eyes out?

"In this case, yes." She glanced around. Spying a towel he'd set out as a dumping spot for muddy boots, she snatched it up and knelt, drying the snow from his feet. "At least I had a jacket and shoes, which is more than I can say for you. Honest to Pete, Alessandro," she scolded. "You haven't changed a bit. For a man who claims to be so logical, you can make the most illogical choices."

"Don't do that."

"Don't do what?"

He caught her by the shoulders and pulled her upward. "Don't touch me like that." The words escaped through gritted teeth. "Don't…don't wait on me."

"Why ever not?" Her eyes were the faintest flash of blue in the dim entryway and a slight smile softened her mouth. "Do you think I'm demeaning myself?"

"Aren't you?"

"Is it demeaning to help? Is it demeaning to warm you after you showed such concern for me? I don't think so." She tossed the towel aside. "And neither do you."

"What the hell is that supposed to mean?"

"I suspect what's bothering you is somethin' far different than my drying your feet."

His senses sharpened, tuned to the hungry give-and-take of her breath, to the song of desire that underscored her words, to the scent of want that perfumed her. He found he couldn't answer. Not that she required one.

"Why can't I touch you, Alessandro?"

The question was an unmistakable provocation, though he doubted she realized it. But he did. He heard the challenge as clearly as if she'd shouted it and he reacted to the subtle mating call on the most elemental level. Sheer, raw instinct took over, rending his facade of calm and stripping all vestige of logic or dispassion. The word that escaped was in Italian, a fiery brand of possession.

He had no memory of snatching her into his arms. No memory of sinking his hands into her hair and tilting her head to a more advantageous angle. No memory of lowering his mouth to hers. All he knew was that one minute she stood apart from him and the next he'd joined her to him with a masculine aggression that couldn't be denied.

He didn't even bother with preliminaries. There wasn't the least need to accustom himself to the slant of her mouth or the feel of her lips or the taste of her. Nor was there any need to ease into the kiss. No initial sampling or exploring. Instead he closed his mouth over hers and plunged inward, demanding a response.

She exhaled in surprise, her breath mingling with his. And then she sank into him, her mouth open and fervent and deliciously hot. She slipped her hands inside his open shirt and splayed her fingers across his chest, warming their chill in the dark tangle of his hair. He shuddered in response. But whether it was from the coldness of her hands or from the delicate urgency of her touch he couldn't tell.

Unable to help himself, he deepened the kiss, voracious in the taking. He'd gone outside to rescue Lauren from her own foolishness. Now he needed someone to rescue him from his. Hunger drove all thoughts from his head, except one. He wanted this woman with a desperation he'd never felt before. Wanted to strip away the ill-fitting clothing and explore every inch of her, from the soft roundness of her breasts to the trim waist and belly to the gentle flare of her hips.

She was willing. Hell, she was eager. If he scooped her up into his arms and carried her to his bed, she wouldn't offer a single word of protest. He sensed she might even welcome it, coming to him with a generous grace unlike any other woman he'd ever had.

Or was that how it had been with Meg? Had she been equally generous in her welcome?

The questions froze him more completely than the snowstorm outside. He swore viciously before he could catch himself. Fortunately, it was in Italian, so he doubted Lauren understood, not that that minor detail made him feel any better about it. His tone had been harsh enough to suggest the intent of his words, if not their meaning. He snatched a quick breath, fighting to recover his equilibrium. Something about the woman in his arms seemed to inspire a loss of control. In fact, he suspected any control he presumed to possess around her was no more than wishful thinking.

"I'm sorry." He set her out of arm's reach, hoping it would be far enough. "I shouldn't have kissed you."

"Why did you?" she asked.

He shrugged, wrapping himself in his illusion of control. "I don't know. Curiosity. Chemistry." His mouth pulled to one side. "Idiocy."

She searched his face. "Are you sure it wasn't something else?"

"To be honest, I suspect it was my feeble attempt to reassure you," he lied without compunction. "You'd been crying. And then you tried to take care of me when it should have been the other way around. I should have been the one offering comfort, not you."

"Comfort." She said the word as though it left a bad taste in her mouth.

He suppressed a groan. Why did women always have to analyze everything—even an impulsive kiss? It must be a genetic imperative. Whatever caused the flaw, it was time to end the conversation before he got himself in any deeper. "I could use a few more hours' sleep. How about you?"

"Nick will be up soon," she warned.

"All the more reason to get back to bed. And I mean you, too." He eyed her critically. "I know exhaustion when I see it. You're not getting enough rest."

"I have a baby to care for."

He took another wild stab in the dark. "It's more than that, isn't it?"

"My sister." The words escaped with an effort. "It's been…rough."

An understatement if he ever heard one. "I have five brothers. I can't imagine having to face what you went through. I hope I never do." He started to reach for her and caught himself at the last minute. Offering comfort again wasn't his best choice at this juncture. It would definitely lead to bed—though not to the sleep she needed so desperately. "You're not alone anymore, Lauren. Consider the Salvatores your family while we figure out why Meg named me as Nick's father."

"She named you because you *are* his daddy."

"Enough, Lauren." He cut her off without compunction. "We've been over that ground. It's pointless to go through it another time when we're so tired. It won't accomplish anything other than to aggravate us both."

She turned her back on him and bowed her head, exposing the nape of her neck. He'd touched the soft skin there, had become intimately familiar with the downy texture when he'd slipped his hands along that vulnerable length into the short, silky layers of her hair. The sensation had been incredible—and one he'd be smart not to repeat.

"I wish there was some way I could help you remember," she murmured.

"Not tonight." His hands balled into fists as he fought the baser part of his nature. "Go to bed, Lauren."

Startled by the harsh demand underscoring his

words, she threw him a startled glance over her shoulder. Shadows cut across her, hiding most of her expression, but not the color or intensity of her eyes. Those damnable eyes. They were the most amazing shade of blue he'd ever seen, and had haunted him since the moment he'd first seen them. Secrets lived there, flitting among the unicorns and Santa Claus and impossible dreams. If he were very, very smart, he wouldn't kiss her again. Hell, he wouldn't even touch her. Because if he did, he'd allow all those fantasies to escape. And if that happened, the results would be catastrophic.

He'd lose every remaining vestige of control.

"Christmas is a'comin'," she whispered a warning of her own. "It's the season for miracles, and whether you want a miracle or not, it'll be here soon."

"You're wrong, sweetheart. This is one place Christmas doesn't visit. And I don't believe in miracles."

Her smile broke through the darkness, along with a soft, silvery laugh. "Oh, Alessandro. You can't stop it. Not with all your logic or all your determination or all your strength. You can't control life. Haven't you learned that, yet? It has a knack for handing out the darnedest surprises. And when it chooses you, your only option is to fight a losing battle or embrace what you're handed with open arms."

"Since you seem to know me so well, I don't have to tell you which option I'll choose."

Her smile dimmed. "No. But that doesn't mean I won't keep trying to change your mind." A yawn caught her by surprise and she stretched with catlike suppleness. "You're right. I am tired. Once I have a few more hours of sleep, I'll have enough energy to keep discussing the situation until you agree with me.''

Alessandro couldn't help laughing. ''I don't doubt that for a minute.''

He watched as she disappeared into the kitchen and chuckled quietly. Discuss the situation until he agreed with her. Hell, one more kiss and she could have claimed they were husband and wife and he'd have been addlepated enough to swear they'd stood before a magistrate and spoken vows.

He headed into the kitchen and on toward his bedroom. No question. That kiss had been a mistake. He hesitated outside her tightly shut bedroom door. Time to make a few decisions in regard to the appealing Lauren Williams. And the first of them would be that he wouldn't touch her again.

After all… He was in complete control.

''Nicky!''

Damn. He should have left a note for Lauren, Alessandro realized a little too late. Her panic the last occasion she woke up to find her nephew missing should have clued him in.

''We're in the kitchen,'' he called. ''We're having breakfast.''

She flew through the doorway, skidding on the slate floor, her arms pinwheeling for an instant. Her frantic movements drew her thin cotton shift taut across her breasts and he shot out his hand to steady her before she could land on her backside. He felt the wiry strength beneath the supple skin of her arm, the compact arrangement of sinew and muscles well accustomed to hard, physical labor. It didn't come as any surprise. Lauren struck him as the sort who spent most of her day working and very little of it relaxing. He'd have to see what he could do to change that during the time she stayed with him.

"Thanks," she said breathlessly, regaining her balance.

He released her, as disgusted as he was amused to discover he'd already managed to break his no touching rule. How long had it taken? Two seconds in her presence? Three? "No problem. Sorry to scare you again. I heard Nick thrashing around in the crib and decided the men would take care of breakfast while you slept in." He swept the boy's little nose with his fingertip. "Isn't that right, buddy?"

Nick greeted the question with a slew of cheerful gibberish, holding out his arms for Lauren's embrace.

She gave him an enthusiastic kiss, oblivious to the oatmeal and yogurt smeared across his face. "I don't usually oversleep."

He didn't need to ask why. "You can't afford the luxury."

"No."

"Well, you can afford it while you're staying here. I'm happy to help out."

She smiled her thanks, looking entirely too appealing for a woman who'd just crawled out of bed after a night of multiple interruptions. Her hair surrounded her head in a rumpled silvery cap and her eyes were still misted with sleep. Although fear had stolen the color from her cheeks, her lips were a rich, striking pink, tempting another kiss.

He deliberately turned back to Nick and shoveled another spoonful of blueberry yogurt mixed with oatmeal into the boy's mouth. "I have coffee or hot

chocolate ready once you're dressed. Any prefer-
ence?''

''Chocolate,'' she responded instantly.

''Marshmallows, whipped cream or plain?''

''Marshmallows?'' She reacted with as much excitement as Nick when Alessandro had produced the
box of toys. ''*And* whipped cream?''

''Tell you what…'' Maybe he could use the opportunity to get some answers. ''I'll put in both if
you'll show me some sort of physical proof that Nick
is my son.''

''Darlin', you've got yourself a deal.''

Without another word, she scurried from the
kitchen. By the time he'd finished feeding Nick and
cleaned up the splattered remains of his breakfast,
Lauren had returned, freshly showered and dressed in
baggy jeans and a loose, pullover sweater. Alessandro
handed over Nick and poured her a large mug of hot
chocolate. He topped it with a healthy helping of
marshmallows and whipped cream. When he passed
her the drink, she shoved a creased photo in his direction. Drinking the chocolate with greedy elegance,
she silently awaited his reaction.

Alessandro studied the picture carefully. It was a
close-up snap of a woman in her early twenties.
Instead of being a short silver-blond like Lauren,
Meg's hair was a bright, glistening gold. And though
her eyes were as dark a chocolate brown as his own,
her appearance was similar enough to her sister's to
suggest a familial relationship. She was quite lovely,
perhaps prettier than Lauren in a conventional sense,
her expression shy rather than impish. Still, they both
shared identical wide, generous smiles and sparkling

gazes, as well as the same triangular-shaped face and delicate features.

"Was her hair long?" he found himself asking.

"Down to her waist," Lauren confirmed, scooping up a dollop of whipped cream with a fingertip and popping it into her mouth.

"And fine as cornsilk?"

She slowly returned the mug to the table. "You do remember!"

"No, I don't." He deliberately set the photo on the table and stepped away. "Is this all the proof you have?"

"Yes, you do," she argued, her tone ripe with desperation. "You remember her. I can see it in your eyes. Something about my sister—"

"Enough!" A trace of an Italian accent flavored his command, one he seemed helpless to control. "A photo is not proof."

Reluctantly, she shifted Nick to the opposite hip and pulled a piece of paper from her pocket, one that had been folded and refolded repeatedly. It was a birth certificate, the copy officially stamped and notarized. She set it on the table and smoothed the creases. "There's this."

He picked it up and scanned the information. The mother's name was listed as Margaret Mary Williams, the space for the father had been left blank. Nick had been born at six-seventeen Christmas morning in an Asheville hospital.

"They don't allow an absentee father to be listed on the birth certificate in North Carolina," she revealed. "Otherwise your name would be there. Alessandro Vittorio Salvatore, as I recall."

"I'm impressed."

"Are you still convinced you're not his father?"

"As I said. I believe you're convinced." He gave the certificate a final glance, freezing when he took another look at the baby's name. "Nick stands for Dominic?" he questioned, stunned.

"Yes."

Aw, hell. He hadn't expected this. "Was that a family name?"

She nodded, drinking down the last of her hot chocolate. "But not our family. *Your* family. He's named after your father, Dom."

"Meg knew my father's name?" he bit out. "How?"

Lauren closed her eyes and released her breath in a gusty sigh. "I've explained how. You just won't believe me."

He didn't dare, regardless of the mounting evidence. "I'd be more inclined to listen if I knew for a fact that Nick was mine."

"You sound cynical," she complained. "And there's no earthly reason for it."

No reason? "You're kidding, right? There's every reason. A stranger shows up on my doorstep, baby in arms and insists I fathered him. Who wouldn't be suspicious or even a little cynical?"

"I take your point. But there's something you should consider before leaping to conclusions." She buried her face in the dark waves of Nick's hair as though drawing strength from his closeness. "I suspect the woman who showed up on your doorstep with that baby in her arms expected you to recognize her. Maybe she has every right to feel suspicious and cynical, too, wondering how it's possible for a man to forget something as significant as fathering a child.

But maybe she respects the man in question enough to withhold judgment until all the facts are in.''

The soft words dropped between them, the depths of anguish they expressed painful to hear. As much as he'd like to explain, he couldn't. Not until he was ready. Not until— *Until what, Salvatore?* Until he had no other option? Until he was convinced of her sincerity? Her innocence? One look had given him a reasonable assessment of her character. He was delaying because he didn't want to raise her hopes, only to crush them again. Or maybe it was because he didn't dare face the truth.

Nick could be his.

''Until I have proof positive, forcing the issue is pointless,'' he said.

She accepted his answer with a stoicism he could only admire. ''You're not going to have proof positive for a while. I assume these tests take time?''

''I have no idea. I'll make a few phone calls today and find out.''

''And if the results take a week or two?''

''Then they take a week or two.''

''You're missing my point.''

She held out Nick and Alessandro relieved her of the baby. He still didn't believe that Nick was his, but that didn't stop him from examining the miniature features, searching for a resemblance. Lauren exited the kitchen and he followed her into the living room. Rummaging through the carton of toys, she removed a selection of balls and plastic books, setting them on the rug next to where Alessandro had placed Nick. The baby immediately grabbed the nearest book and began chewing on it. Lauren flopped down next to him and took it from his mouth. Opening to the first page, she pointed to a picture of a kitten.

"Cat." She smiled encouragingly. "Can you say cat, Nick?"

He flashed his teeth at her, babbling a string of jibberish that didn't sound the least like cat.

"Has he learned any words?" Alessandro asked.

"Not yet."

"Isn't that unusual? I thought they knew a few by the time they were one. I seem to remember Luc's youngest could say—"

Mommy or daddy, he'd almost told her. But right now, Nick didn't have either, poor kid. It was a little hard to learn the words without a source of reference. A line appeared between Lauren's brows and Alessandro silently cursed himself for giving her one more thing to worry about.

"I'm sure it'll come in time," he reassured. "As for what we were discussing before… If you're worried about a place to stay while we wait for the test results, you're welcome to stay here."

"Even if it's over Christmas?"

"Sure. Why not?"

She propped her chin in the palm of her hand, sparing him a quick, assessing glance. "Because Nick and I intend to celebrate Christmas and I gather you don't."

"If you mean a tree and all the trimmings, then no. That wasn't my plan."

"If we stay, you won't have any choice," she warned.

"Sure I will," he corrected. "You won't find any decorations in the house and I'm not going out and buying any at this late date."

"Fair enough."

"I mean it, Lauren. No Christmas. I came here to escape all that."

"I mean it, too, Alessandro. You feel free to spend Christmas your way. Nick and I will celebrate it in our own fashion. If that's not acceptable, we'll find someplace else to stay."

"There *is* no place else," he reminded.

She shrugged, smiling as though she didn't have a care in the world. "Then that's that. Discussion over."

He wished he could believe her. But from what little he knew of Lauren, he was willing to bet the discussion had just begun—a fact she'd explain to him. And if he didn't get it the first or second time, no doubt she'd explain it to him some more until he did. Not that she'd win this particular battle. He was adamant.

No Christmas and that was final.

CHAPTER FOUR

Five days before Christmas...

SHE *came to him again, all silk and sweetness and heady feminine perfume. Escaping their bed, she crossed the room to stare out of the window. Her hair was unbound, flowing down her back to conceal her nudity in a sheet of blush-gold.*

"It's snowing," she said, a note of wonder. "Spring's sittin' on our porch, bangin' at the door and yet, darned if we don't have snow on the ground."

Alessandro lifted onto his elbow and patted the empty space next to him. "All the more reason for you to come back to bed, bella mia. *We can stay right here until the snow's melted and spring comes for real."*

She glanced at him over her shoulder, her dark brown eyes filled with curiosity. "Did you know... Every once in a while you have an itty-bitty hint of an accent."

"I'm not supposed to have one at all."

"Then why do you?"

"Italian was my first language," he explained with a shrug. "We learned it as children at home. My family still speaks it when we're all together. Once you meet them, you'll realize my accent is the least noticeable of all my brothers."

"That's deliberate, isn't it?"

As usual, she seemed to possess the uncanny ability to see right through him, to sense his innermost thoughts and feelings. It should have made him wary. Instead, he welcomed the intimacy and openly encouraged the connection between them. "Yes, it's deliberate."

She approached the bed and he could see her features more clearly now. They were Rhonda's.... And yet, they weren't. Her nose was smaller and straighter than he remembered, her mouth wider and more generous, her chin and cheekbones more elegantly carved.

"Why is it deliberate?" she asked.

"Because it's a weakness."

She tumbled into the bed beside him. "You mean it betrays a weakness, betrays when you're feeling emotional or—"

He swept her into his arms. "Or when I feel like making love to you. Like now."

She grinned. "I'll remember that. In fact, darlin', I intend to take shameless advantage of it."

He couldn't resist, he whispered the words that betrayed him, words of love in a language made for love. And with each new endearment, she unfurled, opening to him like a flower to the gathering warmth of spring.

He was helpless to resist.

Whack!

He wanted her. Whack!

Needed her. Whack! Whack!

Took— Whack! Whack! Whack!

"What the *hell* is going on?"

Alessandro leaped from the bed and crossed to the bay window in two swift strides. The first struggling rays of daylight were penetrating the darkness of the surrounding woods. Another series of whacks came from a stand of trees a short distance away. He couldn't say how he knew, but there wasn't a doubt in his mind that when he went to investigate he'd find a slender elf there. It also didn't take much effort to figure out what she was doing.

He swore beneath his breath, the slew of Italian words infuriating him all the more. It signaled a loss of control. Dammit all! He was supposed to be the dispassionate Salvatore. The analytical one. The one who rarely lost his temper and even more rarely displayed any depth of emotion. Hadn't that been one of Rhonda's chief complaints? According to his dear ex-wife, his passion for life had never equaled hers. Of course, he hadn't been able to equal her abrupt loss of passion, either. Rhonda had a talent for falling in love almost as rapidly as she fell out of it, regardless of whether it was over a job, a hobby, a social cause…or a husband.

Another series of rapid-fire blows had Alessandro dressing with swift efficiency. Leaving his bedroom, he paused long enough to check in on a soundly sleeping Nick and to assure himself that Lauren was indeed gone before striding for the back door. This time when he left the house, he snatched his coat off the rack and thrust his feet into boots.

The sharp crack of splitting wood echoed across the mountaintop as Alessandro stepped outside and he plowed through the snowdrifts toward the source of the sound. He found Lauren in the midst of a dense stand of Douglas firs, his ax slung across her shoulder, grinning triumphantly down at the small tree she'd just felled.

"You are a beauty," she crooned to the poor, helpless evergreen. Grabbing one of the lower branches she struggled backward, dragging it through the snow and talking all the way, the words coming in breathless pants. "Now, I don't want you to feel bad about this. You and I both know you wouldn't have lasted past another year or two. It's much too crowded in here and you were bound to have all your light and water stolen by your bigger brothers and sisters. This way, instead of starving to death, you get to come home with me where you can give my Nicky a beautiful Christmas. Now isn't that a more noble purpose?"

"If it answers back, let me know," Alessandro said dryly.

He hadn't raised his voice and yet the words reported like a rifle shot. Lauren jumped. The ax she'd shouldered tumbled into one snowdrift, while she tumbled into another. She emerged, liberally coated in icy white.

"Oh! Alessandro. I didn't see you there." She slapped snow from her thighs and the seat of her jeans, drawing his attention to her pertly rounded backside. "I thought you were sleepin'."

"I was. For some reason I had trouble."

"Bad dreams?" she asked sympathetically.

"No. It was a rather nice dream." Unsettling, but nice. "Something else woke me."

To his surprise, she went stark white. *"Nicky!"* She floundered from the drift, her normally graceful movements disjointed and awkward. "What happened to him? Is he all right? Is he hurt? I have to get to him.''

He caught her before she planted herself face-first in the snow. ''Easy, *bella mia,*'' he soothed. ''I didn't mean to alarm you. Nick's sound asleep. That's not what woke me.''

''Not…'' She snatched a quick breath. ''Nick's safe?''

''Safe and sound.''

''I—I thought—''

Nothing good, apparently. ''Sorry I scared you.'' What in the world had happened that she kept assuming the worst about Nick? Had he been in an accident she'd neglected to mention? Or was her anxiety the result of the circumstances surrounding her sister's death? He'd have to make a point of asking how Meg had died. Leaning down, he plucked the ax out of the snow, offering an easygoing smile. ''Does this clue you in to what woke me?''

She blinked, understanding finally dawning. ''Oh. My chopping.''

''Yes, your chopping. Mind telling me what's going on?''

She broke into a rapid-fire speech at direct odds with her more natural drawl. ''I was picking out a Christmas tree. Won't cost you a penny or involve any time or trouble on your part, just like I promised yesterday.''

''Lauren—''

She plowed gamely onward. ''It was supposed to be a surprise for when you woke up. If truth be told, I should have gotten to it two days ago. My family always used to cut our tree exactly a week before the big day. But with the snowstorm and everything….''

Her gaze lifted to the magnificent firs surrounding them. "The four of us would go together and spend hours finding the perfect one. Daddy would cut it down. Then in the spring, we'd plant a sapling. He said it was important to give back what we'd taken."

Her comments struck a chord, resonating with familiarity, but he couldn't say why. "I gather you've taken over the job?"

She shrugged. "There wasn't anybody else to do it." A muscle clenched in her jaw. "I'm the only one left."

He hardened himself against an overwhelming wave of compassion. Regardless of her reasons, he wasn't about to let her ignore his preferences. "I thought I'd made my feelings clear about all this."

"You did," she replied, meeting his eyes with customary directness. "Just as I made myself clear about my feelings. As I recall you told me I wouldn't find any decorations in your house and you weren't going out and buying any. Since you don't have to worry about either one of those possibilities, seems to me I stuck pretty darn close to what you wanted."

So much for wearing him down by "explaining" things. Why explain when she could simply walk outside and act on her decision? Apparently the rationalization would take place afterward. "You intend to force the issue, regardless of the fact that it's my house and my choice?"

"Yes." She walked back to the tree she'd cut down and grabbed hold of the lower branches, defiance implicit in every rigid line of her body. "I'm not about to have Nicky celebrate his first Christmas without a tree and all the trimmings. Nor am I gonna let you play Scrooge to your own son. Not when I know you'll live to regret your decision in years to come. Now, you can either help me or stand aside so I can get down to business. But one way or t'other, this tree is goin' in that house. You got that, Mr. Salvatore?"

"Ms. Williams?"

She took a deep breath and braced herself. "What?"

He handed her the ax. "If you'll move out of the way, I can get this done a hell of a lot faster than you. That way we won't risk freezing to death while we discuss our difference of opinion."

It took an instant for his words to sink in. The minute they had, a huge smile spread across her mouth and her eyes glittered jewel-bright. "Thank you, Alessandro."

"You're welcome."

The tree she'd chosen wasn't excessively large, maybe a scrap taller than her own five foot two or three. In fact, compared with some that had graced the cabin in years gone by, it was on the puny side, although it had a pretty shape—rather like Lauren, herself. He understood why she'd chosen it. She'd been correct in her assessment. The tree wouldn't have survived much longer. Grasping the trunk, he swung it onto his shoulder and worked his way toward the house. Depositing the tree by the back door, he shook it briskly to get rid of its mantle of snow and ice along with any loose debris.

"Would you mind heading in and starting the coffee while I rig a stand for this?" he asked.

She peeked at him with the expression he'd come to dread—the one with far too little sensibility and way too much hope. The one full of fantasies and sweet dreams. She wrinkled her nose at him. "No more discussion?"

"I didn't say that." He relented before the fantasies had a chance to fade altogether. "But the discussion can hang fire for a while."

She slanted him a quick, pleased glance, brimming with a gratitude he didn't deserve. "In that case, I'll be happy to fix the coffee."

He caught her arm before she could disappear inside. "I assume the decorations will be next after the tree?"

Her smile faded slightly, replaced by a hint of her earlier determination. "Count on it."

"You're pushing your luck, lady. Nick's only a year old. It's not like he's going to remember."

"*I'll* remember," she retorted fiercely, pulling free of his hold. "This isn't just Nick's first Christmas. It's also my first Christmas with him. And it's going to be one I'll remember for the rest of my life."

He could hear the ripple of emotion underscoring her words, a hint of sorrow, and...and *panic*. It stopped him cold. She was afraid, he realized, stunned. "What's going on, Lauren?" A horrible, gut-wrenching thought occurred. "Is there something wrong with you?"

"I'm healthy as the proverbial horse," she retorted, dismissing the question with a wave of her hand. "Don't you get it? I thought I'd have Nick forever. I thought I'd spend every Christmas with him, every birthday, every holiday, every...every *day*." Tears gave her words a raw intensity. "Ordinary, normal, average days. Days that would stretch into months and years. But when I realized that wasn't possible, that I couldn't raise him alone—"

"You came looking for me, hoping against hope that Meg hadn't lied about our affair and I'd admit Nick was my son." He allowed that to sink in before asking the one question she refused to address, "What if he's not?"

"Don't you get it?" she demanded, fiercely. "Once the proof is in and you find out he *is* your son, you'll take him from me. You have a huge family. Plenty of people to lend a helpin' hand when the goin' gets rough. I don't have anyone to turn to when I'm uncertain. Not a mother or father, not aunts or uncles or cousins, not even my sister. What if I make a mistake? What if I'm a bad mother? I can't take that risk. I can't let my ignorance hurt Nicky."

"That's not going to happen."

She nodded grimly. "You're darned tootin' it's not, because he comes ahead of every other consideration. I'm gonna do right by that boy, no matter how painful those choices might be. Whatever's best for him will have to be best for me, too. I won't—" Her voice cracked, fracturing the still of the crisp morning air as sharply as the Christmas tree she'd felled. It took her a full ten seconds to master the tears that threatened and start again. "I won't let any harm come to him."

With that she whirled around and escaped into the house, leaving Alessandro to stare after her. It didn't take any great insight to recognize that something was going on that he knew nothing about. Her concerns for Nick didn't feel natural. There was an underlying anxiety that bothered him. Something had frightened Lauren enough to drive her from her home in search of a father for her nephew. And if he were smart, he'd find out what the hell it was.

He glared at the Christmas tree, fighting to curb an overwhelming sense of frustration. Dammit all! This situation worsened by the day. What if Lauren was telling the truth? She seemed so certain, he found it impossible to dismiss her claim. What if he'd fallen in love and fathered a child with a woman he couldn't even remember? When he analyzed it rationally, he found it easy to deny. After all, he'd just divorced his wife that particular March. And despite what Rhonda had claimed, he'd once loved his ex with a passion alien to his nature. He'd taken her desertion hard. The last thing he'd have done was dive into another relationship.

But what if that was precisely what he'd done? What if he'd eyeballed this Meg and allowed the Salvatore side of his nature to get the better of him? Granted, it wouldn't have been love at first sight. Hell, that sort of love didn't exist except in the minds of romantic fools. But, lust... Now *that* was a distinct possibility. He'd been knocked off balance by sheer physical need once or twice before. Hell, it had happened yesterday morning with Lauren.

Maybe Meg had caught him when he'd been at his most vulnerable. Having signed his divorce papers, he could have been looking for something—or someone—to fill the void. He might have indulged in a brief, meaningless affair, no matter how contrary to his nature. Considering that his ego had just taken a severe bruising and his state of mind hadn't been in the best shape, he might have done something really stupid. All of which brought about an uncomfortable possibility. Could Nick be his? It stretched credulity, but it was possible, despite his being a fanatic about precautions.

Truth time, Salvatore. It was frighteningly possible, given the factors he'd neglected to mention to Lauren.

Alessandro fixed the hapless Christmas tree with a final glare before surrendering to the inevitable. He needed to finish his discussion with Lauren. Now. While she was still too agitated to evade his questions. Abandoning the tree, he went after her. She hadn't gotten far with the coffee. He found the can on the counter with the lid off and the grounds measured into the filter. She'd neglected to add the water to the coffee machine, he noticed, or even switch it on. There was only one thing that could have distracted her. He grinned. Or rather, one person.

Nick.

For all her concerns about raising the boy, her care couldn't be faulted. Meg had left her son in good hands. Loving hands. Didn't Lauren understand that? Apparently not. Turning his attention to the coffee, Alessandro had the Costa Rican brew perking in no time. As soon as he'd finished, he went in search of his houseguests. Not that he had any difficulty tracking them down. He found Lauren in the first place he checked—in the bedroom she shared with her nephew, getting Nick changed and dressed.

''Why didn't Meg tell me about her condition when she first discovered she was pregnant?'' he asked without preliminaries. ''If we had this great romantic affair, why didn't she call or write or come find me?''

Lauren didn't even look up, but continued to diaper a squirming Nick. She completed the task with practiced ease, her actions gentle, yet firm. Even once she'd finished, her hands lingered on his small foot, as though loath to break the contact between them. She counted each toe twice and Alessandro found something unexpectedly moving about the sight. He doubted she even realized what she was doing, anymore than she realized how much she betrayed with that simple act. He'd never seen such vulnerability expressed so openly.

"Meg tried to get through to you," she said at last.

"How?"

"She left messages at Salvatores." She gave Nick's toes a final tickle before slipping socks onto his feet. "They went unanswered."

"I never got them." When he returned to work, he'd find out why they hadn't been passed along. The excuse had better be a damned good one or he'd tear the place apart, even if it meant shredding his reputation as the "cool, calm and collected" Salvatore. "Why didn't she fly to California to confront me in person?"

"A small matter of expense." She glanced at him over her shoulder, an innate dignity implicit in her bearing, as well as the candor of her gaze. "We're not wealthy people, Alessandro. Meg couldn't just up and jet off whenever the mood seized her. It took me a full month to get to you and I only managed that by working my way across country."

Aw, hell. "I'm sorry. I didn't think." A frown pulled his brows together. "But that still doesn't explain why she gave up. If she couldn't afford to find me in person, why didn't she write or keep calling?"

"Hope can die over time," Lauren explained in a pained voice. "Especially without any nourishment to sustain it. And then, there was my sister's illness. Finding you was put on hold while we dealt with her situation."

"Illness?" This was the first he'd heard of Meg being sick. "What was wrong with her?"

"She died from a brain tumor." The tragic simplicity of Lauren's statement cut deep. As though sensing her despair, Nick abandoned his struggles to free himself and reached out, calling to her in his gruff baby babble. Tugging a shirt over his head, she ruffled his dark hair and hugged him close. "The doctors were kind enough to explain how rare her condition was, right before they sentenced her to a year left to live. She didn't even last that long. Only eleven months. Nick was barely nine months old when she passed."

Far too short a time for a mother to know her child. "I'm so sorry, Lauren."

"Me, too," she whispered.

He didn't force the conversation after that. He couldn't. As soon as they finished breakfast, he buried himself in his study, making phone calls. First on his list was Leo. The mechanic promised that the mountain roads would be cleared by the following morning and once they were, Lauren's car would be first on his list. Next, Alessandro set up an appointment with the local doctor to have blood drawn for the paternity test. A further phone call elicited the fact that the lab results would take a week to ten days, though with Christmas and the New Year approaching, they refused to make any guarantees.

Every once in a while he heard Lauren with Nick, her laughter light and carefree and far too appealing. Despite the sadness that weighted her, Alessandro glimpsed a bubbling enthusiasm breaking free, a sunny brilliance that signaled an end to what must have been a string of dismal, soul-deadening months.

After lunch, Alessandro headed outside while Lauren and Nick napped. It didn't take long to build a stand for the tree she'd chopped down. It was just one pathetic little fir, he reminded himself as he transferred it into the living room. Nothing elaborate or over the top. He could live with that. Hell, the tree looked so tiny in the oversize room, he doubted he'd even notice its presence.

But Lauren did. She spent most of the evening admiring it. Shortly before Nick's bedtime, she danced barefoot around the bushy evergreen with her nephew in her arms, an oversize cotton shirt flaring about her slender, jean-covered thighs.

"It's absolutely perfect. Isn't it perfect?" The overhead lights caught in her silver-blond hair, sparking off the short wayward strands. Between her uninhibited dancing, her wide, winsome smile and her tunic-like top, she appeared more pixieish than ever. "It's the prettiest little Christmas tree I ever did see. Don't you think so, Alessandro?"

"Absolutely," he claimed, burying a grin.

"And the smell…" She inhaled, sighing in delight. "Heavenly. Isn't it heavenly?"

He inclined his head. "It's the essence of heaven."

She spun to a halt, her breath coming in quick, soft pants. "Just wait until you see it decorated. You won't regret bringing it in, I promise. It may be small, but it's got spirit."

"I can't argue with that." Though he wasn't referring to the tree. "In fact, I'd say it had an abundance of spirit."

"How can a Christmas tree have too much spirit?" she scoffed. "It's not possible."

"Lauren."

Her smile dimmed. ''You're not fooling me, Alessandro. I can read between the lines, the same as the next person. But you're wrong about both me and that tree. And I aim to prove it to you. There are five days left until Christmas. You'll see. By the time it's here—''

''Lauren.''

She broke off, burying her face against the top of Nick's head. ''I need to put this little fellow to bed,'' she said in a rush. ''He can hardly keep his eyes open.''

''And then we'll talk.'' He'd waited long enough. ''We're going to settle this once and for all.''

She didn't say another word before darting from the room, but she didn't have to. Her expression revealed more heartache than any person should experience. Great. With one simple demand, he'd managed to kill the spirit of Christmas. Hoping to make amends, he went to the kitchen for some coffee. He started to pour a mug for Lauren, but changed his mind at the last minute. No doubt she'd prefer hot chocolate with a liberal helping of marshmallows and whipped cream. Returning to the living room, he deposited the mugs on the mantel and tossed another log on the fire.

Just as he finished, Lauren joined him by the hearth. ''I need facts and specifics,'' he requested, handing her the mug of hot chocolate. ''And I don't want to hear any nonsense about Meg telling you I was Nick's father and therefore I am. Give me more.''

''You really don't remember your time with us?''

He shook his head. ''Not even a little.''

Her brow puckered in a frown. ''I don't understand, Alessandro. How could you forget a full two weeks of your life?'' Her frown vanished, replaced by an expression of utter pain. ''Unless it was so unimportant to you it wasn't worth remembering.''

He didn't respond to the question implicit in her remark. Nor did he want to add to her distress. But there was a detail she hadn't taken into consideration. ''In case you missed it, sweetheart, you and I exchanged a kiss yesterday morning. You can't deny that you found it as enjoyable as I did.''

''What's your point?'' she demanded defensively.

''If my feelings for Meg were as deep and permanent as you claim, that kiss wouldn't have happened. And it sure as hell wouldn't have gotten out of hand as fast as it did.''

She turned away and drifted toward the Christmas tree, running her finger along the short, spiky needles. ''We discussed all that. You said you were trying to comfort me.''

''Is that why you kissed me back?''

''No,'' she whispered.

Curiosity got the better of him. ''Then why did you?''

There was a long pause before she answered. ''I was hoping it might help you remember Meg.''

''By kissing you?'' he questioned skeptically. ''Not very logical.''

''Neither is the hole in your memory,'' she flashed back, swiveling to face him once again.

This wasn't the time to explain. Not until he'd heard whatever story she'd concocted. ''Skip the speculation and give me the details. You said Meg and I met at a restaurant.''

''That's right.''

He leaned against the mantel, coffee mug in hand.

"And our hands accidentally brushed over a cup of coffee and that was it? Love at first touch?"

"No. My sister was your waitress. She…she fainted. You drove her to the hospital. I worked at the restaurant, too, and went with you."

It was his turn to frown. "Was she ill even then?" he asked gently.

"Yes. Though the actual cause wasn't discovered until shortly before Nick's birth. Not that it would have made any difference. Some things can't be fixed." Lauren's carelessness sat at direct odds with the distress evident in her voice. "My sister's condition was one of those things."

"I really am sorry. I may not remember her or any of the events you're describing, but losing your sister must have been rough."

"Yes, it was." She buried her nose in her hot chocolate. "It still is."

He took a long swallow of coffee as he considered how to phrase his next question. "Was there anyone else in her life? I realize she named Nick after my father, but—"

Anger exploded in Lauren's eyes. "Meg named Nick after your father because she knew that's what you wanted. She knew a lot about you, Alessandro. Haven't you been listening? You two were close. Very close. You told her things you never revealed to anyone else."

His mouth twisted. "If you're referring to her knowledge of my father's name, that's hardly classified information."

"It isn't just the names. It's their personalities, too." She ticked off on her fingers. "Your oldest brother is Luc. He's the responsible one. You're second in line and pride yourself on your self-control. Next comes the twins, Marco and Stefano. You described the strange circumstances surrounding their marriages and how wonderful their wives arc, despite how their weddings came about. Then there's Rocco, the tough guy of the bunch—'' She scowled at him. ''Though he's nowhere near as tough as you. And finally, Pietro. Your mother died when you were a boy and for a brief time you were in foster care. You said it had a traumatic effect on your family.''

''All of that's public information. A good investigator—''

''Does it look like I could afford a good investigator?'' she broke in. ''Or even a bad one? Stop analyzing this with your head, Alessandro. Deny the closeness of your relationship with Meg, if you must. But stop looking for an excuse to deny your own son.''

''The tests—''

''The test will confirm your paternity. But what about everything else I've told you? There isn't a test in the world that will prove to your satisfaction that you loved Meg with all your heart and that she loved you.''

''Maybe because that's not how we felt.''

''Don't say that!'' Lauren deposited her hot chocolate on the coffee table, the ceramic mug striking discordantly against the glass surface. Ignoring it, she crossed to stand before him, her hands balled into fists, her eyes incandescent. The muscles in her jaw worked as she fought to speak. ''You fell in love. You told Meg you'd love her forever. You promised, Alessandro. You promised you'd be back. But you never returned. You left her alone and pregnant.

Where were you? Why didn't you return like you said?''

The raw fury of her questions got through to him as nothing else would have. He should have told her the truth when she first showed up on his doorstep. Perhaps if he hadn't been so wary, so suspicious of her motives, he'd have explained sooner. ''I didn't keep my promise because I didn't remember it.''

''*Why?* Why didn't you remember? How could you possibly forget the woman you claimed to love?''

''Because I was in a car wreck, Lauren. A serious one.'' The flat statement stopped her cold. Or perhaps it was the guttural way he said it, the words so thickly laced with the accent of his ancestors that they were barely intelligible. ''I don't remember any of the time I spent in North Carolina. I don't remember you. Or Meg. And I especially don't remember this great love affair you claim I had. Now do you understand? As far as I know, it never happened.''

CHAPTER FIVE

Four days before Christmas…

SHE *came to him again, all silk and sweetness and heady feminine perfume. As Alessandro watched, the early morning rays crept across the bed, gilding her hair with sunshine. He couldn't resist running his fingers through the silken weight, amazed by the unusual texture. He'd never felt anything like it. The hip-length strands clung, wrapping around him, binding them together in chains more vibrant than gold and more enduring than forged steel.*

As though sensing his gaze, her lashes quivered and she opened eyes that were a dark, penetrating brown, the color unusual in one so fair. They were the exact shade of newly tilled earth, rich and fertile and abundant with life. She smiled at him, her love communicated with a natural ease he envied. Not even Rhonda at her most passionate had expressed herself with such open generosity or undisguised ardor. Everything about the woman in his arms spoke of love—the softness of her delicate, mischievous features, the gentle touch of work-roughened hands, the tender emotion lacing even the simplest of words.

"Alessandro? Are you awake?"

He stroked her cheek with his thumb. "I've been awake for hours. You're the one who's intent on sleeping the clock around."

She wrinkled her nose at the blatant lie. "Never in all my born days have I spent so much time lazing around in bed," she scolded. "It's not part of my nature. You've been a very bad influence, Mr. Salvatore."

"I think I've been an excellent influence. You should laze around in bed more often. That way you wouldn't work so hard."

"I wouldn't bother you except… I couldn't sleep."

"Then let's not sleep." He tucked her more firmly against him. "There are lots of other things we can do instead. Now that the snow's melted, we can find more of those crocuses you like so much. What did you call them?"

"Spring's ambassadors. Lauren calls them little cups of hope."

"I like that," he said gruffly. "I sometimes think there isn't enough hope in the world."

Her laughter teased him. "In that case, it's our sworn duty and obligation to find more. Would that make you feel better?"

"Much. How about a picnic lunch?" he suggested. "There's a little shop not far from here where we can pick up some wine and cheese and a loaf of fresh-baked bread. We could load up a basket, grab one of your quilts and go into the woods where we'll find all the hope we need. How does that sound?"

"I had a bad dream." Her breath hitched in the night air. "About you being hurt and alone."

He cupped her face and reassured her with a lingering kiss. "Don't be afraid, bella mia. I'm not hurt or alone. Not anymore. After my experience with Rhonda, I gave up on love and marriage and fairy-

*tale endings.'' He couldn't hide his amazement. ''And
then I met you.''*

"Do you think we could talk for a bit? Just until I
feel sleepy again?"

"We can do anything you want."

"Alessandro?"

*He wrapped her in a protective embrace. "I'm
here, sweetheart. And I'm not going anywhere. What
did you tell me the other day? Home is where the
heart is? Well, my heart and home are right here with
you."*

"Are you awake?"

He wanted her.

"Can you hear me?"

Needed her.

"Please," she whispered. "Don't send me away."

Took—

"Lauren?" He bolted upright in bed, the dream dis-
solving around him, fading before he could fully
grasp the details. "What…?"

A shimmering light from the windows helped him
track her passage into the room. She paused at the
foot of his bed. "Do you mind if I talk to you?"

"Is something wrong? Is it Nick?" He struggled
to separate dream from reality. It was becoming more
and more difficult with each passing night. "Is he
okay?"

Her smile flashed in the darkness. "That's supposed to be my line, remember?" She crossed to the
bay windows, her ghostly figure caught within the
grasp of a full moon. "I couldn't sleep."

"Did Nick wake you?" He deliberately infused his
words with a threatening tone, striving to ease her

tension with a touch of humor. "You want me to have a talk with the boy and explain the facts of life to him?"

A short laugh escaped her. "No. It wasn't his fault. He's pretty good about sleeping straight through until morning."

Alessandro frowned. That didn't make sense, not considering the well-used path she'd carved between her bed and Nick's crib. "Then why do you get up so often? You must check on him four or five times during the night."

"I'm sorry. I didn't realize I'd been disturbing you." Curling up on the window seat, she wrapped her arms around her legs and drew them tight against her chest. Moonshine draped her in silver, flowing across her hair and cheekbones and down to her shoulders before losing itself in her white cotton shift. She bore an uncanny resemblance to the photo of Meg in that moment, the light giving the illusion of long, lustrous hair. "You have no idea how hard I've tried, but I haven't been able to sleep through the night. So whenever I wake, I peek in on Nick as a precaution."

Alessandro still didn't understand. "Did he just start sleeping an eight-hour stretch? Is that why you're having trouble adjusting?"

"No, he's been doing that for ages. Unfortunately, my disrupted sleep patterns don't have a blessed thing to do with him. Not anymore."

"Then what?"

The confession came reluctantly. "I used to get up every couple of hours to check on my sister. Especially toward the end." She shrugged. "I guess the habit stuck."

It took a minute for the full import of her words to sink in. "Wait a minute. Your sister?" He stared in disbelief. "*You* nursed her?"

"There wasn't anyone else," she said simply. "She didn't have medical insurance and we lived a bit off the beaten path. It was hard to get help. At least, help we could afford. Besides, she found being at home a comfort. How could I deprive her of that?"

No wonder Lauren looked so exhausted. He'd assumed it had come from the difficulty of playing surrogate mother to Nick, or the fact that she'd worked her way across country. But to care for a terminally ill sister on top of the demands of a baby... Hell. It was a wonder she hadn't dropped from sheer exhaustion months ago. "You said Meg died in September. I'd have thought that was enough time for your sleep patterns to readjust."

She rested her chin on her bent knees. "Maybe they would have if it weren't for the dreams."

Her comment struck a chord. "That's right. You said something about having a nightmare when you first came in." He could sympathize. Though his dreams couldn't be termed nightmares, they were disturbing. "Do you want to talk about it?"

She started to shake her head, then hesitated before nodding abruptly. "It's the same one I have almost every night. I've been having it for close to a year." She shivered, her voice so low he could barely hear it. "In the dream I'm all alone and it's snowing. I'm trapped outside in the cold. Bitter, bone-gnawing cold."

"You're not alone now," he reassured gently. "I'm with you."

"Believe me, it helps knowin' that." She laced her

fingers together. There was just enough of a glow from the moon for him to see her knuckles bleach white beneath the tightness of her grip. "Normally the dream doesn't get me quite so worked up. But tonight was different. It…it changed."

"How?"

Her gaze fixed on him. The color had been washed from her eyes, leaving them glittering crystalline-bright within the oppressive shadows. "You were in it this time. I wasn't the one all alone, anymore. You were. You were hurt and no matter how hard my sister and I looked, we couldn't find you." She exhaled, the sound harsh within the gentle embrace of the darkness. "I need to know about your accident, Alessandro. What happened?"

Considering the events of her dream, she wouldn't like what he told her. "According to my family, the day I was due to fly home from Asheville, I ended up in a car wreck."

She struggled to conceal her alarm, with only limited success. "Someone hit you?"

"No. I skidded on a patch of ice coming down from the mountains outside of the city. I went off the road into a deep gully."

He saw the taut movement of her throat as she swallowed. "There's more, isn't there?"

"It took a while for anyone to find the wreck." He kept his voice even and dispassionate. "They say I was trapped in my car for hours."

She buried her face in her arms, shuddering. "Alone and cold. Just like in my nightmare."

"Don't, Lauren." He left the bed and approached, grateful that he'd chosen to sleep in a pair of sweat-pants tonight. She shifted to one side and he took a seat next to her, draping a protective arm around her shoulders. ''If I was cold, I have no memory of it. No memory of being alone, either. No pain or panic or fear.''

''Oh, Alessandro. You may not remember, but you were all of those things. How could you not be?'' She curled into him, wrapping herself in his warmth. ''Tell me the rest.''

''I'm not sure that's a good idea.''

That day had left scars he'd rather not discuss. He'd lost far more than his memory in the accident. He'd also lost an essence of himself, a time line that connected his frame of reference from the days before the accident to the days following it. There was a gap, a lack of continuity that troubled him still and left him feeling out of kilter. But far worse, he'd lost an irreplaceable talisman…the chain holding his mother's wedding band. He still hadn't found the words to tell his father. He doubted he ever would.

''Please, Alessandro. I need to know what happened.''

He hesitated for a moment before relenting. ''According to the report, the accident occurred early in the morning. The rescue workers told Luc that if I'd driven that stretch an hour later, the sun would have melted the ice and the accident could have been avoided.''

''You had to leave early,'' she whispered. ''You had a plane to catch.''

He didn't question how she knew. ''I came out of the coma two weeks later. I remember leaving San Francisco in mid-March. I remember meeting with my wife—ex-wife—and her lawyer to finalize our divorce. And I remember waking in the hospital with a full month missing from my memory. What happened between leaving the lawyer's office and returning to San Francisco is a blank.''

''It's not a blank to me.''

Between the dreams he'd been having and some of the things Lauren had told him, he was beginning to believe it. ''Discussing what happened that day isn't going to help you sleep.'' He thrust a hand through his hair. ''And it sure as hell isn't going to help me get through the night.''

''No, probably not.'' She pulled back ever so slightly and stared up at him, a wealth of emotion in her gaze—sadness, regret, pain…and a heartrending hope. ''Thank you for telling me about your accident. I know you don't remember me. Or my sister. But it's made a huge difference hearing why you never returned. It explains so much.''

''It must have been tough for Meg, especially with her health problems coming on the heels of her last months of pregnancy.'' It was as close as he'd come to conceding that he'd had a relationship with Lauren's sister. But it wasn't the issue that concerned him the most. ''Having the baby's father desert her must have made everything all the harder,'' he forced himself to add.

''*Your* baby, Alessandro. Nick's your son.''

''So you've told me.''

''And you didn't desert him. You'd never have done that.'' She allowed her comment to sink in and Alessandro had the distinct impression he wouldn't like what she said next. ''If you're going to be a proper father to him, he'll need love. So do you, for that matter.''

''There's where you're wrong.'' The correction

came out sharper than he'd intended. "I already tried my hand at love and romance and fairy-tale endings. They don't exist."

"You found them with Meg," she whispered. "You've just forgotten."

He'd had enough. One way or another, this conversation would end. He slipped his hand along the nape of Lauren's neck, stabbing his fingers deep into the silken layers of her hair. Moonlight fell full across her face, gifting her with a breathtaking beauty while dusting him with insanity.

"Did I find love with her? Are you so sure?"

She didn't hesitate for an instant. "Yes."

"Then why don't you try and help me remember the way you did before."

He lowered his head toward hers, inhaling her unique fragrance. He caught the crisp, clean odor of soap mingling with a more distinctive scent—the scent of a baby. *His* baby, most likely. Knowing Lauren carried his mark in such an elemental way stirred something primal in him, as did another, richer aroma that underscored all the others. It was an earthy, feminine essence that interacted with him on the most basic level. It spoke of a desperate want, a want that mirrored his own.

A want he couldn't resist.

The softest of moans escaped her throat. And that's all it took. He breached the tiny gap separating them. The hunger he'd felt for the woman in his dreams vanished beneath the onslaught of what he experienced the moment his mouth collided with Lauren's. Her lips mated perfectly with his, parting to welcome him home. He wouldn't get a better invitation. He surged inward, totally losing himself in the most delicious mouth he'd ever tasted. And then she did something that shattered his self-control.

She touched him.

Just one simple touch and a desire so fundamental, so primitive and powerful seized hold. It wiped out over two full decades of self-imposed restraint as though they'd never been. The work-roughened tips of her fingers danced from the flat plane of his abdomen, over his chest to his shoulders.

"Alessandro, please," she whispered, winding her arms around him.

Hearing his name on her lips impacted with devastating force. He wanted her. Now. He wanted to rip the scrap of cotton from her body and imprint himself on every delicious inch of her. He'd been a fool to think he could control their embrace. Hell, control of any sort was sheer illusion. How his brothers would laugh if they could see what one small, silver-haired elf had managed to do to the Salvatore everyone had considered a passionless aberration.

Not that he was feeling particularly passionless now. Deep, powerful emotions howled through him with more ferocity than last night's storm. Unable to resist, he swept his hand down the length of her spine, contouring her body to his. Lauren shivered in his arms, the eager tremors stealing the last of his self-possession. He surrendered to nature's demand. Tipping her back against the cushions of the window seat, he traced the path of moonlight traversing her shift.

Her breasts were sweetly rounded, peaking under the thin cotton, the dusky centers a tempting hint of darkness beneath a blanket of snowy white. The hem of her gown had ridden up, exposing her lean, pale thighs and hinting at the feminine shadow crowning the apex. It tempted him beyond endurance. So few clothes and so much time. It was a prescription that could only end one way—naked and joined in the best way humanly possible. Few as there were, the clothes had to go. Cradling her hips, he swept his hands upward, peeling off her shift and tossing it aside, leaving her perfectly, gloriously naked.

The moonlight flowed across her, benevolent in its caress, and her pale skin took on a pearly luster, the only darkness marring the satin sheen coming from the inky silhouette he threw across her. The contrast was inescapable. Light and dark. Day and night. Sunshine and shadow. He sketched a finger across her breast, a trail of ebony upon a palette of purity. For some reason the images made him uneasy and he pulled his hand back.

"If you stop now, I'm like as not to scream," announced his palette of purity.

A chuckle shuddered through him. "Ah, *bella mia,* you have such a way with words."

"So do you, Mr. Salvatore. Especially when they're in Italian."

"I don't speak it often."

"No, you don't. Mostly when you're upset. Or so I've noticed."

He lifted an eyebrow, not bothering to ask how or when she'd made that particular observation. "Then why do you like it?"

"Because at least when you're speaking Italian I know you're feelin' something."

It was an opinion he didn't intend to pursue. Not when it was said with such sympathetic understanding. ''Let's see if I can't share some of those feelings,'' he suggested instead.

He didn't give either of them time to think, but came down on top of her, taking her mouth and drinking in her sweetness. Desire washed across her skin, burning him with its heat. Unable to resist, he followed that path of warmth, fitting her breasts in his hands. He could feel the pounding of her heart and he had the oddest impression that he harbored the very essence of her within his grasp.

She was a silvered sprite, a Christmas gift of starshine and moondust and as he gazed down into her soft blue eyes he saw again the unicorns and Santa Claus and impossible dreams. The dreams were struggling to break free, coming to life with each touch and kiss and whispered endearment.

He reared back, fighting to untangle himself from the one place he wanted to be more than any other. What the *hell* was he doing? Had he lost every ounce of common sense? Apparently. There was something about Lauren that drew him, bewitched him. A dangerous passion he couldn't seem to resist. Or perhaps it was simply that he didn't want to resist. Whatever the reason, it defied understanding. He was the logical Salvatore. The passionless one. The only one of Dom's six sons who didn't base his decisions on emotions or gut instinct or any of the other ridiculous excuses his brothers routinely trotted out.

And yet here he was, making love in a window seat to a woman who believed with every fiber of her being in everything he rejected with every fiber of his.

Lauren drew his attention with a gusty sigh. ''You're having second thoughts, aren't you?''

He didn't bother with pointless denials. "Yes."

"I assume we're not gonna make love?"

"You won't scream, will you?" he asked warily, recalling her earlier threat.

"I'll do my level best to contain myself."

"In that case, no. We're not going to make love. It wouldn't be our smartest move."

"Smart." She nodded, as though in response to a question only she could hear. "I guess that means you also won't handle this incident very well come morning, will you?"

"Not even a little."

"That's because you're thinking instead of feeling." She lifted up on one elbow, seemingly oblivious to her nudity, and regarded him with endearing sincerity. "I'm forced to confess, Alessandro, this logic business is one of your most troublesome characteristics."

"It's a defining characteristic, not a troublesome one."

"I suppose that depends on whether or not you're the one spread naked on a window seat."

"If it helps any, I'm not exactly unmoved by that fact," he retorted dryly.

To his surprise, she tilted back her head and laughed. Any other woman would have been furious or tearful or embarrassed. Any other woman would have scrambled to cover herself with whatever came to hand. But not Lauren. A teasing grin played across her generous mouth, encouraging him to share the absurdity of their situation. "There's hope for you yet, Salvatore."

"I'm gratified to hear it," he said with all due humility. "But I'm afraid I'll have to insist that one of us show an ounce of common sense."

"You're probably the best choice for the job. I'd fail miserably."

He reached down and snagged her shift from off the floor. It was far too thin considering the chilly temperatures. She really needed to wear flannel. Layers and layers of thick, all-encompassing flannel. He dropped the shift over her head and tugged it into place. She emerged looking a bit more rumpled, but no less tempting. A tender smile lit her piquant features, a smile echoed in the warmth of her gaze.

"One of these days, I'll get through to you," she warned. "I'll convince you to make a decision based on your emotions, instead of logic or intellectual consideration."

"Let's hope you're wrong."

Her smile faded. "For your sake, not to mention Nick's, let's hope I'm right." She escaped the window seat and started for the bedroom door. The moon no longer tracked her path and with each step she vanished deeper into shadow.

"Lauren?"

She paused. "Yes?"

"Just so you know... The paternity test is scheduled for tomorrow. We'll learn the truth about Nick by the New Year."

"No, Alessandro. I've found the truth has a way of winning out, whether we want it to or not. You'll know everything by Christmas. I've decided to make it my gift to you."

Damn. "And here I didn't get you a present," he murmured.

"What you can give me is very simple." Her

words slipped through the darkness, the cadence a rich, rolling reminder of her mountain homeland. "And it won't cost you a plugged nickel."

"Something tells me it's going to cost me a hell of a lot more than that."

"You might not want romance in your life, but Nicky needs a father's love. That's all I want for Christmas. I want you to love again."

He hadn't left the window seat and moonlight continued to pour down on top of him, leaving him totally exposed to her scrutiny. He struggled to keep both voice and expression aloof. "You're asking the impossible."

"Am I?" Compassion formed a base for her question. "I don't think it's impossible at all, darlin'. You just don't remember how to go about it."

She spoke with a certainty that had nothing to do with rationality and he combated it with the only weapons he had at hand. "And you're here to remind me? With sex, if necessary?"

"That's right." Her teasing laugh annoyed him. There was nothing the least amusing about any of this. Their situation called for calm reason, not half-baked promises or any other touchy-feely get-in-touch-with-your-feminine-side sort of bull. She opened his bedroom door. "You will let me know when I succeed, won't you?" came her parting shot.

She disappeared into the hallway, leaving him fighting for control. "You can count on it," he whispered. "Though I suspect you'll figure it out long before I realize what's hit me."

"Please, Lauren. Don't cry."

"I'm not crying," she instantly denied, a ragged sniff giving lie to her claim.

"Then what's all that stuff leaking out of your eyes?" Alessandro stooped low enough to catch a droplet with the knuckle of his index finger. "It sure looks like tears to me. I swear, you're the cryingest woman I ever have met."

"I am not. It's just…" She started to touch the colorful adhesive bandage decorating Nick's arm and yanked her hand back, fresh tears welling into her eyes. She smothered the top of his little head with a flurry of kisses. "I can't bear it when he gets his shots. And this was even worse. It's a wonder they didn't suck him dry."

"Worse for you than for him, I suspect. He only fussed for a minute."

"He's brave." Her breath caught on a sob and she fumbled in her pocket for a tissue. "Very, very brave. Poor darlin'."

Alessandro thought fast, desperate to come up with some sort of distraction. "Would it help if I bought you an ice cream?"

A reluctant smile broke through her tears. "Nick's the one who had his blood drawn. Not me."

"Yeah, well, Nick isn't the one in tears." He took the boy from her, tucking him in the crook of one arm while dropping the other around Lauren's shoulders. "My mom used to dissolve into tears anytime one of the six of us was injured. She'd get so upset, we'd end up comforting her."

"You were all wonderful sons to be so caring," Lauren claimed loyally.

He shook his head in remembered disgust. "And

then Dom would go out and get her a little something to cheer her up.''

''What about you boys?'' A hint of indignation infused her voice. ''Didn't you get anything?''

''Oh, sure. The wounded one would get—wait for it—ice cream.''

Her gurgle of laughter pleased him no end. ''That explains your suggestion.''

He couldn't begin to guess why he'd told her the story about his mother. He'd never told anyone, not even Rhonda. It was a part of his life he didn't often think about. It dredged up far too many bittersweet memories. ''Come on. We'll have a cup of coffee to warm us and a dish of ice cream to make us feel better.'' He didn't bother reaching for his chain. This time he remembered that it wouldn't be there. It didn't keep him from silently saluting his mother's memory. ''Consider it honoring a family tradition. A very special tradition.''

They passed a flower shop on the way to the restaurant and as soon as they'd been seated in the small café, Alessandro excused himself and slipped outside. The trek back to the florist only took a minute, the purchase less than that. He worked very hard not to analyze his actions. Returning to the table he put the small flowerpot in front of Lauren.

She stared at it for the longest time, an odd expression on her face. ''You bought me crocuses.''

''So I did.''

''They're *purple* crocuses.''

''True.''

''Spring's ambassadors,'' she murmured.

Alessandro grinned. "Nah. They're little cups of—"

His grin faded and his grim gaze locked with Lauren's.

"Hope," he finished softly. *"Damn."*

CHAPTER SIX

Three days before Christmas...

SHE *came to him again, all silk and sweetness and heady feminine perfume. Alessandro sat in the middle of chaos watching as she sorted through the "bounty" she'd collected from the woods. Leaves, pine needles and pinecones, twigs and vines were scattered around her.*

She looked liked a pagan goddess amidst a circle of charm, her hair flowing to her hips in a river of gold, her strong, slender body moving gracefully from pile to pile, sorting with practiced assurance.

Alessandro watched in admiration. Life with this woman just got more and more interesting. "So what, exactly, do you make from all this?"

"Critters," she replied.

"Critters," he repeated, his brows drawing together. "What are those?"

Laughter gleamed in her dark eyes. "Look around you, boy. They're all watching. Waitin' for me to bring more of their kind to life."

He started to question her again, then broke off and did as she said. And that's when he saw them. "Critters" were everywhere. Deer peeked from the middle of plants. Grumpy dwarves guarded the logs stacked by the fireplace. Mischievous elves cavorted under the furniture. Bashful woodland creatures hid out of the way in shadowy corners.

"How could I have missed them?" he marveled, crossing to take a closer look at a miniature herd of deer. They'd all been made from the materials she'd collected from the woods. A small stag with an impressive rack of feather antlers sat askew and Alessandro gently straightened it.

"You missed them because you're so busy thinking, you forget to be quiet and look. You'd be amazed at how much more you learn when you stop tryin' to analyze and just let things come of their own accord and fill you up."

He lifted an eyebrow at that. "Fill me up?"

She rocked back on her heels and studied him with an expression that reflected her rich, indomitable life force. "Inside, Alessandro. Where you're needy. Everything around here is whispering to you, tryin' to tell you their special secrets."

He went to her, scooping her clear of her collection. "Tell me your special secrets," he demanded.

"They're surrounding you, darlin'." She wrapped her arms around his neck, her head nestling against his shoulder. "Home is where the heart is, remember? Look at my home and you'll see my heart."

"Just keep reminding me," he ordered gruffly. "One of these days I might get it."

"I'll remind you for as long as you love me. I promise."

"Then that will be forever."

She lifted her mouth to his and he was helpless to resist. He wanted her. Needed her.

Took her.

* * *

Alessandro found the first Christmas decorations when he got up the next morning. They'd appeared sometime during the night and were a series of miniature "stick" animals, unquestionably in the shape of Santa's reindeer. Whiplike branches had been artfully laced together to form a frame for the torso, head and legs, while bits of moss and pine needles had been woven in to add definition to each animal. Holly leaves were used for antlers, cotton balls provided tails, and on one of them a bright red berry formed its nose. The lead reindeer had been left slightly askew and he automatically corrected its position.

The creations were clever and whimsical and Alessandro knew with every fiber of his being that he'd seen something similar before. The memory lay just beyond his reach, buried within the darkness of the weeks he'd lost that long-ago March when spring had finally eclipsed a stubborn winter. But no matter how hard he fought to summon an inkling of those missing days, he couldn't tease them from their hiding place.

It was driving him insane.

Selecting one of the figures, he tracked Lauren to the bedroom she shared with Nick. "I recognize this," he announced, carefully setting her creation on the handmade quilt she'd spread across the mattress. Even that looked familiar and he deliberately turned his back on it. No question. He *was* going insane. "Tell me where I've seen it before."

She cast him a hopeful glance, the same one she'd had the day before at the restaurant. He'd expected a torrent of questions then, but she'd surprised him by not asking any at all. Her restraint had impressed the hell out of him. She utilized the same restraint now, though it appeared more strained around the edges than yesterday. He'd have to explain soon. After what she'd revealed about her dreams, she deserved to know about his.

"My sister and I used to make them," she replied, passing him Nick, a plastic diaper and a warm, damp washrag.

He took the hint. If she thought he'd balk at changing a baby, she had a lot to learn. Ever since his nephews had grown numerous enough to require a calculator to keep track of them all, he'd been in the unfortunate position of having to take a turn or two at diaper duty. Although he'd abdicated the job whenever possible—what man wouldn't?—he still knew how to address the basic fundamentals. He scowled at the diaper. Maybe. Trying to decide which side to use for the front and which to use for the back might prove more of a challenge than he'd expected. But he was an intelligent, college-educated man. He could figure it out.

Lauren reached around him and flipped the diaper over. "That way," she murmured.

"Okay, okay. So I need a little help," he groused. "The minute I return to civilization I'm going to write a letter to the manufacturers suggesting they draw arrows on the damn thing or stamp directions on the bottom. That way it won't be so confusing."

"Can't see what for. Men never read directions, anyway." Laughter rippled through her voice. "Just take your time. I have every confidence in you. After all... A man as calm, cool and logical as you shouldn't have any problem with an itty-bitty diaper, not to mention an itty-bitty boy."

He jerked his head toward her bed, pointedly

changing the subject. "Did you bring the reindeer with you or is this a recent creation?"

"Recent. I've been working on them at night whenever I can't sleep." She crossed to the dresser and opened and closed drawers, sorting through the limited stacks of clothing. "I find it…soothing."

"Still having nightmares?"

"Oh, they're improving," she replied brightly. "Now we're both trapped outside in the cold. But at least we get to share the experience."

"A definite improvement." *Smart move, Salvatore.* Just what she needed, to dwell on her nightmares because he was too stupid to keep his mouth shut. "So… Where do you find the supplies to make your stick figures?"

"My sister and I used to go into the woods and gather bits and pieces of trees and plants for the various designs. Some I brought with me and others are native to the area around here. I managed to collect them before the storm hit."

Alessandro finished stripping a surprisingly cooperative Nick, grinning when the boy's chubby legs began to pump with a surplus of energy. "Like being naked, do you, buddy?"

Lauren chuckled as she watched. "You'll find out how much he likes it when you try puttin' his clothes on. He can be downright ornery on the subject of getting dressed, so prepare yourself for a tussle."

"As you said, how much trouble can one little kid be?" Alessandro scoffed. "Besides, we have an understanding."

"Sure you do. And you'll find out what that understanding is the minute you try stickin' a diaper on his backside."

He buried a grin. "So what are they made from? Your reindeer, I mean. Sticks?"

"Sometimes, if they're pliable enough. Mostly we use cane, vines and bark. Twigs. Pinecones and pine needles make a nice touch. So do berries. I've found nature has an abundant warehouse to choose from." She pulled socks and a T-shirt from the drawer, followed by a pair of corduroy pants and a long-sleeved shirt with snaps along the shoulder. "Tonight I'll work on Santa and his sleigh. Or maybe I'll string popcorn and cranberries for the tree."

"You like all this Christmas stuff, don't you?"

"Darned right." She hugged Nick's clothes to her chest and turned to check on his progress. "I gather you don't?"

"Not even a little. That's why I come up here and use the cab— Damn!" Moving with impressive speed, he ducked out of harm's way. "Seems your nephew's sprung a leak."

"Oh? Didn't I warn you about that?" she asked a little too innocently. "I've found a warm washrag does prompt surprising results. Good thing you have such excellent reflexes."

He shot her a quelling glance over his shoulder. Lauren fought to maintain a straight face, not that she fooled him. She found his predicament funny as hell. "Keep it up, lady, and I'll teach him how to improve his aim. Then we'll see how successful you are at staying dry while you change a diaper."

"I'll take you up on that offer when it's time to potty train him." The words hung between them, words he knew Lauren would have taken back if she could. She stared at him, stricken. "Alessandro—"

"Potty training sons is definitely a father's job,"

he replied in an even voice. "If Nick's still around then, I'll be happy to take care of it."

Without another word, Lauren crossed to the bed and curled up on the quilt. She'd placed the tightly furled crocuses he'd bought her in a spot of honor on the nightstand table, and she reached out to run a finger along the rim of the flowerpot. It took several seconds of effort to steel herself enough to look at him. But once she had, her gaze met his with familiar directness. "I apologize, Alessandro. It wasn't my intention to keep on at you about the subject."

"Forget it. I realize it wasn't deliberate."

"That's kind of you to say so." She shoved her fingers through her hair, adding to its slightly rumpled appearance. "I have to tell you, the sooner those test results are in, the happier I'll be."

"That makes two of us." He tickled Nick's tummy. "Three if you count this guy."

Returning his attention to the task at hand, Alessandro wrestled with Nick's diaper. He managed to wrap it around the boy's plump, squirming hips, but only after a prolonged struggle. A string of baby babble gave vent to Nick's disapproval of the process, along with the rapid-fire hammer of small, painfully accurate feet. Corraling the boy with a firm hand, Alessandro looked at Lauren and inclined his head toward the quilt spread beneath her.

"Your sister made that, didn't she?"

The words dropped between them, taking on growing significance with each passing moment. The flowerpot rattled against the table and Lauren jerked her hand away. She stared at him, her emotional turbulence changing her eyes to a deeper, more vivid shade of blue. "You *know!*"

"Just answer the question. Did your sister make the quilt?"

There was the briefest of hesitations before Lauren nodded. "Meg made it, yes. But how did you—"

"If you'll finish dressing this little guy, I'll get breakfast started." Alessandro picked up Nick and carried him to the bed. It was time for that discussion. Past time, if he were honest. He wanted to tell Lauren the truth. *Needed* to. The dreams he'd been having provoked too many questions. With luck, she might be able to answer one or two of them. "I can explain while we eat."

A short while later, Lauren entered the kitchen, her expression more strained than when she'd first arrived. Alessandro turned off the burner beneath the griddle, cursing himself for a fool. He shouldn't have been so abrupt before leaving. He should have taken an extra few moments to reassure her. No doubt her imagination had been running riot the entire ten minutes it had taken her to join him.

"Relax, Lauren. It's nothing bad." He took Nick from her and installed him in the high chair. "Just something I should have told you before."

She didn't appear convinced. Without a word, she slipped into the seat opposite his. He heaped a steaming stack of pancakes on a platter and placed it in the middle of the table along with a jug of maple syrup. "Is there any reason Nick can't have some?" he addressed her bent head.

"He loves pancakes," she murmured. "Cornbread, too."

"I'll keep that in mind."

Pouring two cups of coffee, he added a generous spoonful of sugar to Lauren's for her sweet tooth, along with a shot of cream. "I've been having these strange dreams for a long time," he began without preamble.

Accepting the coffee, she slanted him a surprised look. "Dreams?"

His mouth curved in a humorless smile as he joined her at the table. "You're not the only one who isn't sleeping well. Although I can't categorize these dreams as nightmares, they're…unsettling."

She took a moment to digest that. "Go on," she urged, taking a hasty sip of coffee. "What do you dream about?"

"In every one, it's springtime." He cut up a pancake for Nick, dabbed it with syrup and let the boy have at it. Piling a plate high, he passed it to Lauren. "But even though it's spring, there's snow on the ground. There are also crocuses, strangely enough."

"Purple ones, right?" she interrupted eagerly. "Like the ones you bought yesterday."

He nodded in confirmation, voicing the suspicion that had been troubling him for the past several days. "That's one of the things that happened in North Carolina, isn't it? Meg and I found crocuses in the snow."

"Yes."

"She used to call them spring's ambassadors. While you nicknamed them 'little cups of hope.' That's what I was remembering in the restaurant yesterday."

"*Yes!*"

"And we had a picnic." Now that he'd started, he couldn't seem to stop, the words torn from him. "In the woods."

"You spread the quilt beneath a huge oak," she

encouraged. "The quilt in my bedroom. The one you remembered Meg had sewn. What other things do you dream about?"

He shrugged. "Playing hide-and-seek in the woods. Making love. The picnic on the quilt. We ate bread and cheese and drank wine."

"Those are all things you did with Meg." Excitement quivered in her voice. "What else?"

"Her voice. Laughter."

She closed her eyes, concealing her thoughts from him. He didn't have any difficulty guessing what they were. The slight tremble of the coffee cup in her hands was a dead giveaway. She set it carefully on the table. "You remember," she whispered. "You *remember*! Why didn't you say anything before?"

"Because these aren't memories, Lauren. They're dreams."

She rejected his assertion with a wave of her hand. "I don't see much difference."

He leaned across the table toward her. "I'll tell you the difference. I don't trust dreams to accurately reflect reality. For all I know it could be my subconscious playing games as a result of my accident." Polishing off the last of his pancakes, he gestured for her to do the same. "You're not eating any better than you're sleeping. You can't keep going the way you are without eventually paying a price for it."

He half expected an argument. But other than an irritated shrug, she obediently tackled the pancakes. "Why didn't you tell me any of this before?" she asked after a few minutes.

"I thought the woman in the dreams was my ex-wife, so I didn't see any point in mentioning it."

She considered that for the length of time it took

her to consume another pancake. "Just how long have you been havin' these dreams?"

"Close to a year."

Lauren gave him an odd look. "A year this next March?" she guessed shrewdly. "Exactly a year from the date of your accident?"

He gave her full marks for perception. "I don't know about exactly. But they started sometime this past spring, yes."

Pushing her plate aside, she took a swallow of coffee, regarding him through the steam coming off her cup. "And these dreams were about Rhonda?"

She knew his ex-wife's name, and yet, Alessandro knew for a fact he'd never identified Rhonda by name to Lauren. It was one more bit of proof that his life had been entwined with the Williams family at some point. "No. I *thought* I was dreaming about my ex. At least, she was the woman occupying center stage until recently. That all changed when you showed up."

Lauren returned her mug to the table with a clatter, the coffee sloshing over the rim. "I don't understand."

"Ever since you arrived the woman has changed until now she looks remarkably like the picture you showed me," he confessed. "But that could be my imagination playing tricks on me. The power of suggestion."

Nick chose that moment to indicate he'd finished his breakfast. Throwing his uneaten pieces of pancake onto the floor, he leaned over the high chair and eyed the messy results with satisfaction. Then he held out his arms toward Lauren. "Ma-ma," he said in a clear, piping voice.

"Interesting." Alessandro looked at Lauren and cocked an eyebrow. "Something you'd like to tell me, sweetheart?"

"Yes. As a matter of fact, there is." Lauren lifted Nick from his high chair and clasped him close, sticky fingers and all. "Consider yourself blessed. You just heard your son speak his first word. I wish my sister had lived long enough to do the same."

With that, she swept from the room, leaving Alessandro invoking every Italian curse he could remember, along with a few he invented on the spot. "One of these days I'll learn to keep my damned mouth shut," he muttered. "Too bad it couldn't have been five minutes ago."

Alessandro made a firm vow to avoid raising any more controversial issues. He even took the time to write it down, in case he made the fatal mistake of forgetting again. Lauren spent the afternoon creating additional stick figures and stringing popcorn interspersed with cranberries, while Nick did his level best to wreak havoc every step of the way. Deciding to play it smart for once, Alessandro didn't utter a single complaint about the decorations. Worse, he found himself making excuses to wander through the room as each new "critter," as he'd privately dubbed Lauren's creations, made an appearance. He straightened one of the reindeer that once again sat askew on the mantel and tried to analyze their appeal. They added a festive warmth and charm to the room, he decided, a warmth and charm that held serious appeal.

In the middle of the afternoon, he found her out for the count on the couch. Nick played nearby, yawning sleepily. Scooping him up, Alessandro carried the boy into Lauren's bedroom and wrestled a clean pair of diapers onto his uncooperative backside, relieved to discover that when he'd finished they were taped on the right way. Finally, he tucked Nick into his crib, and watched in amazement as the little guy popped a thumb in his mouth and went straight to sleep.

Alessandro left the room feeling disgustingly pleased with himself. Now why had his brothers taken such delight in regaling each other with the horrors of baby care? This daddy stuff was a snap. There could only be one explanation. Using logic and reason rather than blind emotion must offer hidden benefits. He'd make a note to mention it to the others.

With time on his hands to spare, he closeted himself in his study and placed a call to his brother, Luc. "I've been wondering when you'd break down and phone," the oldest of the Salvatore boys growled. "You have some explaining to do."

"Not that it's any of your business," Alessandro retorted dryly.

Luc snorted. "Yeah, right. A slip of a woman shows up at Salvatores with a baby in arms, asking for you and it's none of my business. Let me tell you, I had a nasty moment of *déjà vu* there."

Alessandro didn't doubt it. Their brother, Pietro, had gone through a similar experience, only in his case the baby had been dumped in Luc's arms while Pietro had set out to find his former lover and convince her to marry him. The incident had almost ended in disaster, especially when child welfare had become involved. It had also led to Luc marrying his secretary, Grace, an outcome that had delighted all the Salvatores.

"Do you have any idea how hard it's been keeping the news from Dom?" Luc continued. "Pietro's almost slipped up twice. He says welcome to the club, by the way."

"Tell Pietro to go to hell." Alessandro straightened in his chair as Luc's initial comment sank in. "Dad doesn't know, does he?"

"Not yet. But it's only a matter of time. Come on, little brother. Spill. What's going on? Or do I have to beat the answers out of you?"

"Let me repeat. It's none of your business." Alessandro relented, aware he didn't have much choice. "But since you've asked so nicely, I'll tell you. I don't know whether Nick's mine. I can't remember the incident in question, the woman in question, or how she could have talked me out of using any form of birth control. And before you ask, yes, we're doing a paternity test. The results will be in before the end of the month."

"Nick? That's the kid?"

Alessandro released his breath in a long sigh. "Nick. As in short for Dominic."

"Damn."

"My thoughts exactly."

They both fell silent for a moment. And then Luc spoke up again. "How the hell can you forget fathering a baby? Or perhaps the better question is... How can you forget the woman you fathered him with? She looked pretty memorable to me."

"It happened in North Carolina. And Lauren's not the mother, she's Nick's aunt."

Luc groaned. "Let me guess. Your missing few weeks just turned up."

"Or so Lauren claims."

"Convenient, if you ask me."

For some reason, Alessandro found himself jumping to Lauren's defense. "I believe her, Luc. She's positive Nick is mine."

"You don't think it's a scam?"

"I thought so at first."

"But not any longer?" Luc persisted.

"Not on Lauren's part, no." Not for one little minute. "How truthful the sister was is another question altogether. Once the test results are in we'll know for sure."

"What was this sister's name?"

"Meg. She died a couple months ago. Lauren's been taking care of Nick ever since."

To Alessandro's surprise, Luc responded in Italian, the word he used short and explicit and very crude. "Listen, little brother," he began uneasily. "There's something I might have forgotten to tell you about those days you were in the hospital. This might be a good time to mention it."

A sense of inevitability slid over Alessandro. "What did you forget?"

"You called out a woman's name."

"I don't suppose it was Meg?" he asked dryly.

Luc cleared his throat. "Now that you mention it. Meg does have a familiar ring to it."

"I thought it might."

Silence reigned. Then Luc asked, "What are you going to do?"

What could he do? "I'm going to take it one step at a time."

"And if Nick is yours?"

Alessandro remembered what Lauren had said the night he'd first kissed her, her words as much a warning as a promise. *"Christmas is a'comin'. It's the season for miracles, and whether you want a miracle or not, it'll be here soon."*

"Then Lauren will be right," he replied softly. "Christmas will be a season for miracles, whether I want it or not."

But somehow he suspected he wanted this particular one, wanted it with a surprising desperation.

CHAPTER SEVEN

Two days before Christmas…

SHE *came to him again, all silk and sweetness and heady feminine perfume. They'd finished the bottle of wine, eaten bread and cheese until they were replete and fed the remaining scraps to a curious gray squirrel and an eager flock of robins. Stretching sleepily, she sprawled on top of a patchwork quilt, the colors an appealing splash of springtime pastels against the gold of her hair. It was chilly beneath the shade of the oak and Alessandro wrapped his arms around her to keep the cold at bay.*

With a teasing smile, she slipped her icy hands beneath his shirt to warm them. He sucked in a pained breath and took it like a man. "Better?" *he managed to ask.*

"Much." *Her fingers began a tantalizing exploration. Eventually they encountered the chain and ring he wore around his neck and she tugged at it.* "What's this?"

Removing the chain, he handed it to her. "The ring belonged to my mother. She died when I was ten."

The light dimmed in her dark eyes. "I'm so sorry."

He shrugged. "Don't be. It was a long time ago. I barely remember."

"Don't bother lyin' to me, Alessandro. You

wouldn't still be wearing her ring after all these years unless it meant something to you.''

"Habit." The word sounded abrupt even to his ears.

"Can't you tell me what happened?'' she asked gently. "Does it still hurt so much?''

He couldn't begin to guess how she knew. "My father put that chain around my neck the day we buried my mother. It was just after Christmas.''

"Oh, no. Not Christmas.'' Her hands slid around his waist and she hugged him. "First your momma, then Rhonda. No wonder you don't like that time of year.''

"She died the week before the holidays.'' It was a relief to tell her, something old and painful easing within him as he talked. "Dad was in Italy on a business trip. My youngest brother, Pietro, was a newborn. After she died Luc tried to take care of us all. But he was only fourteen and child welfare finally stepped in. We were placed in foster care until Dom could be notified and get home.''

"Did they keep you all together?''

"No. There were six of us. Too many for any one home to take in.'' He felt a suspicious moisture dampen his shirt and frowned. "Hey, you're not crying, are you?''

She shook her head. "No,'' came her muffled response.

He didn't believe her. Hooking her chin with his finger, he lifted her face to his. "You are crying.'' He couldn't remember anyone ever crying for him… except his mother. But then, she'd cried over everything. "Don't, sweetheart. It's ancient history. No harm done.''

She swiped at her cheeks. "I can see the scars, even if you can't," she maintained fiercely.

"Little scars." What phrase did she always use? He pinched his fingers together. "Itty-bitty scars."

"You shouldn't carry any scars at all." Her tears lessened and her expression grew lighter. Gently, she returned the chain to his neck. "Maybe we can get rid of some of them."

"And how do you propose to do that?"

"Let's see...." She rolled on top of him and rested her forehead against his, winding her fingers deep in his hair. "Do you know what today is?"

"Not really." He caught her mouth in a quick kiss and then laughed. "That's strange. I really don't know. That's never happened before."

"Well, let me tell you. It's the first day of spring. A time for new beginnings. What better day to heal old hurts?" Her hands dropped to the opening of his shirt, plucking buttons through holes. Her eyes were dark and loving and filled with a soft feminine generosity. "Let me heal you, Alessandro."

He was helpless to resist. He wanted her. Needed her.

Took her.

"Alessandro? I need you."

He followed Lauren's voice into the kitchen. "What's up?"

She stood gazing down at Nick, who sat in the middle of the floor, pots, pans, lids and an assortment of wooden utensils spread out around him. She didn't appear happy. "I've decided," she announced in a brave voice. "It's time."

"I'm almost afraid to ask. Time for what?"

''Nick's hair has gotten too long.'' From the way she said it, he'd have thought it was the worst possible tragedy. ''I have to…to—''

''Cut it?'' Alessandro suggested, taken aback when she swiveled to glare at him. ''*What?* What did I say wrong?''

''Don't you dare make light of this.''

''Who's making light of it?''

''A baby's first haircut is a milestone.''

''A milestone long overdue, if you want my opinion.'' Apparently she didn't, since her glare grew more fierce, promising serious retribution. He pitched his voice to soothe. ''Honey, you'll be doing the kid a favor.''

She folded her arms across her chest. ''A favor.''

''Right. He's supposed to be a boy, but with all those waves and curls he's starting to look a bit—'' A quick glance at Lauren's expression had him back-pedaling. Fast. ''Not that there's anything wrong with looking a bit— But you have to agree. He *is* a boy.''

''Thank you kindly for pointing out the error of my ways.'' Boy, he hated when she went seriously Southern on him. Nothing cut worse than words that sounded sweet enough to rot teeth, while somehow managing to flay a man alive. ''I need scissors if I'm gonna correct my parental incompetence.'' She held out her hand as though she expected him to produce them from thin air.

''Tell you what. You get the scissors. They're in the medicine chest in the master bath, and I'll have a little pep talk with Nick. We'll be ready for you as soon as you get back.'' He didn't even attempt to argue the ''parental incompetence'' part. There wasn't a chance in hell that could lead anyplace he wanted to go.

She opened her mouth to argue, but to his everlasting relief she changed her mind. He didn't plan to ask how he'd gotten so lucky. The minute she'd trotted off, Alessandro folded his hands across his chest and fixed Nick with a man-to-man look. "That was a close one."

Nick indicated his agreement by picking up a wooden spoon in one hand, and a pot lid in the other. Showing off his eight pearly teeth in a wide grin, he banged the spoon and lid together, thoroughly pleased with the clatter he created.

"Okay, little buddy. Listen up. It's time for another first for you. This one's going to be a breeze. Not for your—" His brows drew together in a frown as he considered how best to finish his sentence. Then his frown eased. There was only one description that fit. "Not for your momma. This won't be anything close to a breeze for her. More like a hurricane, which means highly destructive and accompanied by a heavy downpour."

"Ma-ma," Nick crowed, banging the lid with even greater enthusiasm.

"Right. I suspect she'll cry her way through each tiny snip, but don't let that scare you. It's a woman thing. As you get older you'll find there are a lot of women things you'll have to deal with."

Alessandro unbuttoned his shirt and tossed it over a nearby chair. Stooping next to Nick, he removed the boy's shirt, as well. "Your best bet is to hold your peace and let them cry it out. Trying to rationalize tends to make women mad, as you might have noticed by that stellar example I just set. You don't want to do that. And using logic only makes them madder. You *definitely* don't want to do that. Or argue." He winced. "You're too young to hear what happens then, but trust me. It's very, very bad."

"Ma-ma." Nick crashed the wooden spoon against the pots and pans. "Ma-ma. Ma-ma. Ma-ma."

Alessandro whistled softly. "I gotta hand it to you, buddy. Once you finally learn a word you stick with it."

Leaving Nick to his Ringo Starr imitation, Alessandro rummaged through the recycle bin by the backdoor and pulled out a layer of newspapers. He spread them in a broad circle on the kitchen floor. "Okay, Nick. Now remember what I told you," he instructed. "No fussing. It'll give your momma the perfect excuse to never cut your hair again. And we can't have that. Don't get me wrong. I like the opposite sex just fine, but we don't need to look like them. A man should look like a man."

Setting a chair in the middle of the papers, he continued his lecture. "Also... While fussing is a no-no, so's grinning. Try not to act too happy. No point rubbing in the fact that she should have done this months ago and you're pleased as punch that she's finally gotten around to it. Are we clear about how to handle this?"

Nick stared with such an intent expression, Alessandro could have sworn he understood every word. Unable to explain what drove him, he held out his arms. Nick used the leg of the chair to lever himself upward and then he threw himself into the embrace. He carried a scent unlike anything Alessandro had ever smelled before—fortunately, not that of a dirty diaper. He'd had close and personal contact with that particular odor over the past few days. A little too close and personal for comfort.

No, this was entirely different. A unique fragrance filled Alessandro's nostrils, something fresh and young and earthy. Something distinctive. Something he hadn't taken the time or opportunity to register before, perhaps because he'd been so careful to hold himself at a safe distance, reluctant to establish any sort of intimate contact. But he wasn't safe any longer and Nick's scent flooded his senses, changing his perception of the boy.

It was almost as though he'd imprinted Nick's essence on some primal level, claiming it as his own.

This was his son.

"Gracious, Alessandro." Lauren hurried into the kitchen carrying a pair of scissors and a comb. "Have you seen the size of that master bathroom?"

He reluctantly released Nick, not quite sure what had just happened. He fought for equilibrium, fought to make sense of an irrational instinct. But coming to terms with any sort of instinct was well outside of his realm of experience. "The master bath?"

"It's huge." She suddenly noticed their state of undress and her eyes widened. A betraying flush brightened her cheeks and a feminine awareness gleamed in her gaze, a hunger that gave him far too much satisfaction. "There's… You know. A—a tub," she continued a trifle incoherently.

He buried a smile. "Most bathrooms have them."

"Yes, well." She made a swift recovery. "Did you also notice it's big enough to swim in?"

"It's a whirlpool tub. For soaking."

She appeared instantly intrigued. "The sort that blows water at you and swirls around?"

"That's the kind. Have you ever bathed in one before?"

"Never in all my born days."

"Would you like to try it?"

She lit up, her wide smile stealing away any lingering traces of stress and exhaustion. "You wouldn't mind?"

"Be my guest."

Her smile dimmed slightly. "I'm not sure." She fussed with the scissors and the comb. "It seems a frightful waste of water."

He made a decision then and there. No matter what it took, he'd get her into that tub. And he'd make sure she filled it to the brim and whirlpooled herself into a cute little pixieish prune. "I think we can spare the water this once." He took a seat and settled Nick on his lap. "We're ready, but I can't promise how long he'll be this calm. Let's get started."

As he'd predicted, the tears started right up. "Do you really think he needs—"

"Yes, I really think he needs." He fixed her with a steely gaze. "And if you can't bring yourself to do it, I'll take over."

"No, no," she insisted bravely. "It's my responsibility."

She crossed to the sink and filled a glass with warm water. Returning to where they sat, she dipped the comb in the water and gently worked it through Nick's baby curls. Picking up the scissors she fussed for a solid three minutes before making her first snip. Alessandro caught the curl as it fluttered toward the floor. It rested in the palm of his hand, appearing incredibly small and silky. He hadn't expected to be affected by the moment. After all, it was just a haircut. But he found something about that one tiny lock of hair unexpectedly moving.

He held it out. "You'll want this for his baby book."

The tears fell in earnest then. "No. You keep it for yours. His daddy should have the first one. I'll save the next."

"Thank you." The words came out gruffer than he'd intended. "I'd like that."

The rest of the haircut proceeded faster and easier than he'd expected. Lauren cried her way through it, but Nick didn't squirm or fuss or protest in any way. Instead, he sat solemnly, watching the entire procedure with the same intense curiosity he'd displayed while listening to Alessandro's instructions. When they were through, Lauren dusted the stray hairs off the two of them and helped Nick into his shirt before returning him to his pots and pans.

"I'll do you next," she told Alessandro unexpectedly, wiping the last of the tears from her cheeks. "You're looking a bit shaggy around the edges."

"That's all right. I can wait until I get back to San Francisco."

"No, I'd like to do it."

He didn't argue. "Be my guest."

She dipped the comb in the water again and drew it through his hair as she had with Nick. There was something unexpectedly sensuous about her movements, the languid pull of the comb, the soft warmth of her breath caressing his jaw, her slow, easy movements as she shifted from one position to the next. He could smell the soap on her skin and the faint hint of herbal shampoo she'd used that morning.

Her breasts shifted beneath her sweater and he

closed his eyes, remembering their sweet weight in his hands. He wanted her. Here. In the kitchen. It was crazy. Nick played no more than three feet away and all he could think about was stripping the jeans off Lauren's hips and yanking the sweater over her head before tumbling her to the floor and making love to her.

Desperation prompted him to speak. "My mother used to line us all up and cut our hair." He couldn't say what sparked the memory. But at least it took his mind off Lauren and what he'd like to do with her. "Luc would sit there the way Nick did and let her get it done. The twins would make her life a misery, hiding in every nook and cranny they could think of until she dragged them out by the ear."

"That's Stefano and Marco?"

"Yeah." He didn't even bother questioning how she knew anymore. "Then they'd turn on the charm. Not that it worked. Momma knew how to handle the Salvatore charm. After all, she'd had years of experience with Dom."

"And the rest of you?" she prompted, snipping cautiously around this ear.

"Pietro was just an infant, so he escaped the lineup. Rocco would perch on the edge of the chair and scowl, hoping to intimidate his way out of it."

"And you? What did you do?" she asked with gentle compassion. "No, don't tell me. You'd try and reason with her."

"The entire time she was hacking away. I don't think I ever shut up."

"I'm sure she loved every minute."

"She probably did." He rubbed a hand across his brow. "I still miss her."

"She sounds like a wonderful mother."

"She was." He had difficulty asking his next question. "Was Meg a wonderful mother? Did she…" He exhaled roughly. "Did she resent having to raise Nick alone?"

Lauren's snipping took on new urgency. "Nick was the most loved child in the world. He still is."

"You haven't answered my question. Did she resent what happened between us?"

The scissors fell silent and he wished he could see Lauren's expression. "Meg never resented her relationship with you." A blunt honesty underscored her words. "Nor did she resent Nick or the need to raise him alone. She felt…confused. And perhaps, for a while, betrayed."

"I'm sorry," he said simply.

"It wasn't your fault. And Nick compensated for a lot of heartache."

"You want me to change the subject, don't you?"

"If you wouldn't mind."

"Okay. Have I told you how much I like your critters?" The scissors made a hasty clipping sound and her gasp sounded close to his ear. Aw, hell. "Problem?" he asked crisply.

"No. No, no. Everything's just fine."

"I can't glue the hair back on after you chop it off."

"True. Fortunately, you can grow out any small errors of judgment."

"How small an error of judgment?" he asked ominously.

"Small. Tiny. Itty-bitty." She cleared her throat. "So… You like my critters, do you? I didn't realize you knew what they were called."

"You could say it came to me in a dream. And I like them very much." He hadn't expected to, but to his surprise, he found their whimsical charm appealing. Santa and his reindeer held the place of honor on the mantel, the one in front often sitting askew. It had become a secret game between them, with Lauren shifting the deer out of alignment, while he straightened it whenever he passed. "I keep wondering where your next creation will crop up."

"I'm surprised you even noticed."

"I didn't at first, not until I had the oddest feeling I was being watched. I finally located the rabbits peeking at me from under the couch. It took me a while to find the flock of sparrows roosting on top of the wall clock." His favorite, though, had to be the family of elves, cavorting among the pine boughs covering the coffee table. They never failed to provoke a smile. "The one I haven't figured out yet is the woman under the Christmas tree. Is it going to be a crèche scene?"

"You'll have to wait and see," she replied.

"Cryptic."

"Personal."

"Even more cryptic."

"I'll tell you what…" He had the sneaking suspicion she was trying to change the subject again. "I'm going to make some more ornaments later today. Why don't you lend me a hand?"

"No." The word escaped more abruptly than he'd planned, but he couldn't help it. "Not a chance."

"Why?"

He used her excuse. "It's personal."

Silence descended, broken only by Nick's determined drumming. "Maybe I can guess."

"I don't think so." There wasn't a chance in hell he'd told Meg this particular story. It went too deep, hurt too much.

"If I do, will you help?"

"Sure." He sounded entirely too flippant, but he couldn't seem to help himself. "Why not?"

"Okay."

She didn't say anything more, but concentrated on cutting his hair. Her fingers shifted through the layers. Smoothing. Soothing. Caressing. It took every ounce of self-possession not to snatch her into his arms. He wanted to feel her hands on him again, taste her sweetness on his tongue, see every inch of pale, silky skin glowing in sunlight as it had beneath the moon's softening rays.

"I think it has to do with when you were in foster care."

Damn.

"I think while you were there they tried to get your mind off your loss by involving you in their Christmas traditions."

He caught her wrist and pulled her around to face him. "How the *hell* do you know about that?" The scissors clattered to the floor. He fought for control as he picked them up and set them out of Nick's reach. But for once that control eluded him. Fury— along with a soul-corrupting torment—overrode every other thought and consideration. "And don't tell me you got it from Meg. I wouldn't have told her the story. I wouldn't have told anyone."

"They were paper snowflakes," she continued in a quiet, steady voice. "Each of the children was sup- posed to cut one out. Then you were going to dip them in heated wax and sprinkle glitter over the top.

Once they'd cooled you each could hang your ornament on the tree. It was a silly activity. Much too young for a ten-year-old. Didn't they realize that? Didn't they know anything? Heck, they even made you put your name on it like you were some snot-nosed kindergarten kid or something."

It came roaring back, as bleak and dark and painful as if it had just happened. "Shut up, Lauren," he whispered hoarsely. "Just shut the hell up."

She didn't shut up, each word pounding like a blow from a sledgehammer. "You did what they asked, but inside you were furious, your emotions more out of control than they'd been in your whole, entire life. They were all laughing and havin' a grand old time. Jokin'. Making you celebrate Christmas when all you wanted to do was go and hide in a dark corner. You were alone and scared. Your mother was dead. The police had taken you from your home, even though Luc had started a fistfight with them in order to keep you all together. Your family had been broken up and your brothers were each sent someplace different. And no one knew where to find your father. Maybe he had died, too, and they were keeping it a secret from you. On top of all that, these strangers were insisting you cut out a bunch of stupid paper snow-flakes."

"You win, okay? I'll make your damn ornaments." Anything to stop her. He gritted his teeth to keep from howling. "Just end it. Now."

But she kept going, slashing toward that dark place, forcing light on a time that held nothing but shame and despair. "It was your turn to dip the snowflake. You can't remember clearly what happened next. You've always wondered whether it was an accident or deliberate. Your foster parents claimed it was intentional, that you were too methodical and precise to have spilled the wax by mistake. Whatever the truth, the pan flipped and their five-year-old son was burned.''

''They took him to the emergency room. He had to spend Christmas in the hospital because of me. *Because of me!*''

''You paid for that, Alessandro. Dear heaven, how you paid. You were placed in a facility for juvenile delinquents until your poppa came for you.'' Tears welled up and trembled on the ends of her lashes. ''You spent Christmas there. A ten-year-old child who'd just lost his momma was locked up like a criminal. Isn't that punishment enough?''

''It's in the past. I don't have to deal with it anymore.''

The tears fell, sliding down her cheeks. ''Don't you get it? You're still dealing with it. You've never stopped.''

''So Christmas isn't my favorite time of year. So what?'' That had to be the understatement of the century. ''I told you that when you first arrived. That's why I come to the cabin. That's why you and Nick shouldn't be here.''

''You come here to hide from the memories. Because you lost your mother at Christmas. And twenty-some years later your wife walked out on you, also at Christmas.''

Ever so carefully he unwrapped his fingers from around Lauren's wrist. His hold must have been crushing, yet she hadn't uttered a single murmur of protest. What if he'd left bruises? Her skin was so pale and delicate. He'd never forgive himself if he hurt her. "Rhonda said Christmas was a time for passion. And that she'd lost all passion for me. She said she couldn't live with such a cold, barren man."

"Rhonda was wrong."

"No, *bella mia*," he gently corrected. "She was all too right."

"Why? Because you've bought into her viewpoint? Because everyone thinks you're the unemotional Salvatore? The calm, cool, logical one?"

"Yes."

"It's a popular opinion, but it's not true." She straddled him. Sitting on his lap, she covered his mouth with her fingertips before he could argue. "You know full well that ex-wife of yours fell in and out of love faster than a round-heeled woman with a string of sugar daddies. You also know that you've gone out of your way to maintain a facade of emotionless logic in order to protect yourself. You've encouraged that opinion in order to conceal the truth. Why, you're the most passionate of all the Salvatores."

He couldn't help it. He laughed, the sound rough and edgy. "Now I'm positive you're crazy."

She released her breath in a long sigh. "Rhonda's passion was fleeting. No doubt it always will be. But yours is forever. That's why the wounds slice deeper, because the emotions are so powerful. That's also why you've worked so hard at self-control. You're afraid of what might happen if you ever turned those emotions loose. You might hurt someone. You might send a small boy to the hospital again." She cupped his face. "But it wasn't your fault, Alessandro. Do you hear me? It was an accident. Those people had no business putting a grief-stricken boy in the vicinity of hot wax. It was disaster in the making. Nor do I believe for one little minute that it was deliberate. You had five brothers, most of them younger. Would you have *ever* done anything to harm them?"

"The boy wasn't my brother."

"I see. So you wouldn't have hurt Pietro or Rocco or the twins, but any other little fella was fair game?"

"You know that's not what I meant!"

"You can't have it both ways. Either you were a nasty little tyke who took joy in harming others. Or you were methodical and precise under normal circumstances, but careless this time because the circumstances were far from normal. Which is it?"

"Don't you get it? *I don't know. I can't remember!*"

"Yes, you do. It was an accident. You just won't admit it because it gives you the barrier you need to hold your emotions at bay. It's like the chain and ring you used to wear around your neck." She stabbed his chest with her index finger. "It was the keeper of your pain, the container for any feelings you didn't want to claim. It held the death of your mother and the injury of that little boy and a wife who didn't understand the depth or complexity of the man she married. That ring and chain protected you. Now that you don't have those circles of protection anymore you're forced to deal with feelings you've avoided for years."

He didn't want to hear any more. Couldn't bear to hear any more. Not when each word rang with such savage truth. He silenced her the only way possible. Thrusting his hands deep into her hair, he sealed her mouth with his.

"Does this feel like I'm avoiding anything?" He

took her mouth again and again. "Or this? Or how about this one? Is that emotionless enough for you?"

"No." Lauren sounded decidedly breathless. "I think you're expressing your emotions just fine."

He reached down to cup her bottom and tug her closer. Her thighs wrapped around him, encasing him in warmth. He wanted her, even more than he had earlier. He fisted his hands in her sweater, about to rip it off. Behind them Nick pounded on his pots with renewed enthusiasm, startling them both. For a long moment, they sat frozen, sanity slow to return. Gradually the desire ebbed, leaving only regret in its wake.

"We can't do this," Alessandro muttered. "Not here. Not like this."

"Not with Nick looking on, you mean."

"No. But it's not just him." The air gusted from his lungs, his breath sounding as ragged as Lauren's. "I shouldn't want you so badly. But I do."

She stared in confusion. "I don't understand. Why shouldn't you?"

"You know the answer to that. Think about it."

Her eyes widened with sudden comprehension and she wrapped her arms around him, burying her face in his shoulder. "Meg," she said simply.

"Yeah." The specter of nine long months' worth of dreams played in an endless reel through his head. "Meg."

CHAPTER EIGHT

The night before Christmas…

SHE came to him again, all silk and sweetness and heady feminine perfume. She was quieter today than he'd ever seen her, the incandescence of her joy dimmed by some worry she refused to explain. He didn't press. They hadn't known each other very long and he suspected that had a lot to do with her reticence. Trust came with time. Unfortunately, they didn't have much to spare. In the few remaining days they had together she not only needed to trust him, but to learn that he was steady and dependable and above all, safe.

He grimaced. Maybe she'd have an easier time believing in him if he hadn't told her so many stories about his father and brothers and the legendary Salvatore charm, none of which tended to inspire a feeling of either trust or safety in women.

She spent the afternoon creating her latest "critter" while he helped by cutting lengths of wire and sorting through the various piles to find the choicest leaves and twigs and pine needles for her to use. He enjoyed working with her, sitting near her, exchanging the occasional look and touch and kiss. After a couple hours her creation took shape. It was a famous trio of monkeys, he realized, wryly amused. Hear no evil, see no evil, speak no evil.

What had she said the other day? "Everything around here is whispering to you, tryin' to tell you their special secrets." He didn't have to listen too hard to hear this particular secret.

"I gather they represent our relationship?" he asked.

She didn't look at him, her focus on the monkeys. Stubborn woman. "Maybe."

"Okay." Patience, he reminded himself. Patience was a virtue. A damned annoying one, but still a virtue. "Let's try this another way. What is it you don't want to hear?"

His tactic worked. The movement of her hands lost their graceful symmetry. "How long, Alessandro?"

"Until I leave?"

"Yes."

"Five more days." He asked the next question. "What is it you don't want to see, sweetheart?"

"Your car." He had to strain to catch the gruff words. "Vanishing down my drive."

"And what is it you don't want to say?" he continued tenderly.

"Goodbye." A teardrop splattered on her worktable. "I don't think I could hardly bear it if I heard that word come out of your mouth."

"Then it won't."

Her head jerked up and she glared indignantly. "You'd be rude enough to leave without so much as a 'see ya later, darlin', it's been swell'?"

He buried a smile. "I have something a little better in mind than that."

Suspicion darkened her eyes. "What?"

"How about this…." He leaned closer, his mouth against her ear. "I love you, sweetheart. I love you

today. I'll love you tomorrow. And I'll keep loving you for the rest of our lives.''

His sincerity broke through her barriers, the fear and reticence and suspicion slipping from her gaze. She came to him with sweet generosity, laughing and crying and whispering all the words she'd kept from him that morning. Desire flared, as it always did between them, and he lifted her into his arms and carried her toward the bedroom.

He was helpless to resist what she so unstintingly offered. He wanted her. Needed her.

Took her.

Alessandro glanced over at Lauren, his brows drawing together. Dammit all! After doing her level best to avoid him all day—not to mention the discussion he'd attempted to start on four separate occasions—she'd capped off the evening by curling up on the couch after dinner and falling sound asleep.

She still looked like a woman who'd been through hell and back, though the tension etching her features had eased significantly from when she'd first arrived. The past year must have been unbelievably difficult. Knowing that he'd contributed to her burden bothered him more than he cared to admit, and as soon as the paternity test confirmed that Nick was his son, he intended to redress that omission.

Nick played with his usual self-sufficient intensity on the floor between the couch and the fireplace and Alessandro used the opportunity to surreptitiously continue with his current project—one he found more difficult than he could have imagined. He'd almost finished the first stage and just needed a quick hour of privacy to complete the final details.

A small noise distracted him and he glanced casually toward the couch again, before coming out of his chair with a bellow. *"Nicky! No!"*

He hit his feet running, diving for his son at the last possible instant. Scooping up the boy, he rolled away from the fireplace and curled his body around Nick, protecting him from the crushing weight of the folding fireplace screen as it came smashing down on top of them. Intense heat burned through the glass-and-steel frame and Alessandro thrust it off him with a sharp blow of his elbow. Beneath him Nick howled in fear.

Lauren reached them before Alessandro could gain his feet, kicking the screen further out of the way before literally ripping the flannel shirt off his back. "Nicky?" she questioned tersely as she examined him.

"He's fine. Just scared." He stood gingerly, flexing his muscles, his son still clasped tight in his arms. Aside from a sore elbow and shoulder, both of which felt more muscular than burn-related, he didn't think he'd sustained any real damage. "That was close."

"Too close. Kitchen," Lauren ordered. Plugging the kitchen sink, she filled it with cold water, dropping in a handful of ice cubes. Pushing Alessandro into a chair she inspected his injuries. "They're not bad. You're a little red, but I think you got the screen off before it could give you a serious burn. We'll try some cold water compresses and put burn ointment on and see how it looks in an hour. If it starts to blister, we'd best get you to the hospital."

"The emergency room is the last place I want to be on Christmas Eve. I'm sure it'll be fine."

She didn't comment on his observation. For the

next fifteen minutes, she tended to him while he comforted Nick. It wasn't until she'd finished and they'd returned to the living room that he got a good look at her. For all her calm efficiency, she appeared hollow-eyed and stricken, but she wasn't crying. Amazing. It took him an instant to realize why.

"You think this is your fault," he accused.

"It is." Her jaw set. "I fell asleep. If I'd been watching Nicky like I was supposed to, this never would have happened."

"Last time I checked, there were two adults in the room, remember? I knew you were asleep. The responsibility is mine. All mine," he emphasized.

"Nicky could have been—"

He cut her off without compunction. "Stop it, Lauren. We're not going there. It was an accident. He's safe. And I'll survive, too." He retrieved his shirt from in front of the hearth. The buttons had all popped when she'd ripped it off him rendering it useless and he tossed it aside. "It didn't occur to either of us that Nick would try and pull himself up using the fire screen. From now on, we'll be more careful. Right after Christmas I'll have the screen changed from a freestanding one to something attached directly to the hearth. Until that gets done, we'll ace out any more fires."

She started shaking then. Delayed reaction, no doubt. "I messed up," she insisted, clutching Nick close. "This time I really messed up."

Nick squirmed for release. Aside from the word, "Ma-ma," his gruff bass litany of complaint defied comprehension, but the tone came through loud and clear. Alessandro retrieved his son and put him on the floor well away from the fireplace. He didn't seem any the worse for their small crisis, though if his aunt didn't calm down, that could change.

"Use some common sense, honey." He kept his tone low and reasonable, the way he did whenever his brothers overreacted. Inspecting the fire screen, he noticed that one of the glass panes had split from Lauren kicking it over. He set the folding panels carefully in front of the hearth, hoping the heat wouldn't shatter the cracked glass before the fire died and he could dispense with the screen altogether. "Try and put your emotions aside and examine the situation logically. We've both looked at this stupid thing any number of times and neither of us thought it posed a danger."

"I should have realized."

"Really?" He threw her a quick glance over his shoulder. "Why you and not me?"

"Because..." She took a deep breath. "Because I know he has a tendency to pull himself up on whatever's handy."

Alessandro shrugged. "I know that, too. I've seen him do it often enough. If either of us had thought the screen was a hazard, we'd have discussed it with each other and decided how best to baby-proof against a possible accident. On top of which, I noticed that you'd fallen asleep and had the choice of either watching Nick myself or waking you."

"But—"

"I took on the responsibility," he argued. "That makes the fault mine. End of discussion."

"At least tell me what's going to happen when you find out Nick's your son."

He didn't have a clue what she was talking about. "I don't see the problem."

"What will you do?" she persisted.

"I'll take responsibility for him. Did you think I wouldn't?" He crossed from the fireplace to confront her. "Dammit, Lauren. You know me well enough by now to realize I'd never desert—"

"Alone?" she interrupted. "Will you raise him alone?"

His brow furrowed. He still couldn't figure where she was going with this. "As you've pointed out several times, I have family who will be more than happy to help."

She swallowed visibly and presented him with her back. "Of course."

Her words were uttered with heartrending stoicism. He understood then and cursed himself for a fool. "Did you think I'd take him away from you?" He caught her by the arm and swung her around to face him. "Because of *this?*"

"It does happen. Children get taken away all the—" Her voice broke and she covered her face with her hands.

"You're the only mother he has," Alessandro soothed. He snatched up a tissue and pried her hands away. Cupping her chin, he dabbed at her eyes. "I'm not going to separate the two of you. I promise. We'll work something out."

She took the tissue from him and scrubbed away the tears. "You don't understand," she insisted fiercely.

"There's nothing to understand. If there's one thing you should know about the Salvatores, it's that we believe family sticks together. That includes you." She didn't argue, but he had the distinct impression he hadn't convinced her, either. He let it go. There'd be plenty of time to reassure her over the next couple of weeks. "Come on. There's something I've been meaning to do all day."

"What?"

He'd succeeded in distracting her. Lifting Nick in one arm, he wrapped his other around Lauren's shoulders. "I've been meaning to thank you for cutting my hair."

She regarded him with wary suspicion. "And how, exactly, were you plannin' to do that?"

"I have the perfect way."

She disengaged his arm and took a hasty step backward. "This is because of my itty-bitty mistake, isn't it?"

"Yup."

"What are you gonna do to me?"

He grinned. "I'm going to strip you naked."

"Oh, heaven be merciful," she breathed. He couldn't quite tell if the prayer was meant to protect her or if it was an endorsement of his plan.

"And then I was going to dump you in that swimming pool that passes for a bathtub and give you an hour of privacy to soak."

"Oh." Her tone turned disgruntled. "I was afraid you had something a tad more scandalous in mind."

"Afraid or hopeful?"

Her mouth twitched. "Maybe a bit of both."

"For your information, I'm not upset about my hair. It'll grow out." With luck, by next Christmas. "As for that something scandalous... Once Nick's in bed, we'll have all night to scandal away."

She nodded. "Thank goodness for that. You had me worried for a minute there."

"That I wouldn't have my wicked way with you?"

"Nope." She peeked at him from the corner of her eyes. "That I'd gotten stuck with the dud of the Salvatore clan."

He was delighted to see her sense of humor returning. "I'll see what I can do to restore my reputation," he assured, duly chastened. He shoved open the door to the master bedroom. "Well? How about it? Are you interested in a bath? I'll put Nick to bed while you go paddle around the tub. There's a sack of books around here somewhere if you want to read. I think we can even rummage up some candles and bubble bath."

The longing expressed in her blue eyes was almost painful to observe. "A bubble bath?"

Aw, hell. "Don't tell me you haven't had one of those, either?"

"The cabin back home doesn't have a tub. Just a shower. But I have had a bubble bath. My daddy rigged one for me and my sister in our cistern. The bubbles didn't last long. But while they did…" A wide, blissful smile spread across her face. "It was heaven."

"That tears it. Bubbles it is." He dropped a quick kiss on her lips. "We'll have our discussion afterward."

"Discussion?" A frown darkened her expression. "What discussion?"

"The one you've been avoiding all day."

Her mouth tugged downward. "There's always a catch, isn't there?"

"In this case, a very small one," he consoled.

It didn't take Alessandro long to get Lauren installed in the tub. Next, he prepared Nick for bed. Last of all he turned his attention to the project their

fireplace disaster had interrupted earlier, hoping he'd
have time to complete it before Lauren was done
soaking. His luck held, though not by more than a
couple of minutes. He'd just put the finishing touches
on it when a piercing shriek came from the direction
of the bathroom.

It was almost an instant replay of his rescue of
Nick. He came out of his chair with a bellow and hit
his feet running. Racing flat-out through the master
bedroom, he slammed open the bathroom door and
nearly took a header as his feet went skidding through
a three-inch river of water.

"What the *hell* is going on here?" Alessandro demanded. Foam rolled across the tile like a sea of
snow, forming drifts to his waist.

From the center of the highest mound in the middle
of the floor, a bubble-capped head appeared. "Help!
I can't get your tub to turn off. I just dumped a bit
of bubble bath in the water and look at what hap—"
Lauren's feet slid from under her and she disappeared
beneath the onslaught of suds. *"Alessandro!"*

"Push the damn off button!"

"I couldn't find an off button," she wailed. "I
don't even know how I turned it on. You forgot to
give me directions."

More bubbles foamed outward in a cascading
wave, stranding a flailing mermaid at his feet, her
only claim to modesty a few strategically placed tufts
of froth. He plucked her off the floor before she could
be washed away and waded through the water to the
huge sunken tub. Reaching through the roiling foam,
he pushed the pressure plate that served as an off
button. The hum of the motor died and the bubbles
stopped multiplying.

Alessandro's arms tightened around Lauren. Finally. He finally had her where he wanted her. "Time for that discussion I've been promising you," he warned.

Huge blue eyes peeked out through a tantalizing mask of suds. "Maybe I should put some clothes on first."

"Don't bother. They aren't necessary for what I have in mind."

And then he kissed her, deciding that maybe a bit of scandal was what they both needed tonight. Her lips softened, parting beneath his. He wanted her. With every day that passed that want grew to something stronger and more powerful than anything he'd ever experienced before. Bubbles clung to him, dampening his shirt and jeans, not that he cared. But Lauren shivered with cold.

Reluctantly, he released her and wrapped her in a thick bath sheet, draping another over her head. Then he raided the linen closet and dumped a pile of towels on the floor to absorb the water and soapsuds. A more thorough cleanup could wait until morning. Satisfied that the tile wouldn't be damaged, he scooped Lauren into his arms again and carried her into the living room.

She stared at him in bewilderment for a moment before she finally noticed what he'd brought her to see. "Oh, Alessandro," she whispered. "What have you done?"

"What I should have done long ago," he said, letting her go.

Clutching the towel to her chest, she crossed to the Christmas tree and touched the dozens of paper snowflakes that hung from every bough. Each had been dipped in wax and sprinkled with glitter. And each had his name written on the back in a bold, dark print. ''They're beautiful.'' She spun around and flew into his arms. ''Thank you, thank you. You couldn't have done anything to make me happier.''

He wrapped her up tight. ''Merry Christmas, sweetheart. Though I hope I can come up with one or two more things to please you.'' But not yet. First they'd have a discussion. ''I've been wanting to talk to you all day and you've been going out of your way to avoid me.''

''Have I?'' Her voice was muffled against his shirt.

''Quite a trick considering we're both living under the same roof.'' He tugged the towel off her head and combed his fingers through the damp strands. ''You're running scared, aren't you? It's the only reason I can come up with to explain how you've been acting.''

Her chin poked out an inch. ''I don't know what you're talking about.''

''Liar. I'm talking about that kiss in the kitchen yesterday. I'm talking about what happens between us every time we get too close.'' He deliberately ran his hand down her arm, eliciting a helpless shiver. ''You forced me to confront some painful truths yesterday. Are you going to make me do the same with you?''

''Please, Alessandro. Not now. Can't this wait until the test results are in? Or at least until after Christmas?''

He shook his head. ''No. I want the discussion before then. I want to have it while everything is still uncertain, so we're dealing with just the two of us and none of our other concerns. Not Nick. Not whether or not I'm his father, though you've convinced me I am. Not even our past.''

''What do you want from me?''

''I want to know how you feel. I want to know if there's a chance for us.''

She gave him a direct look. ''You mean romantically?''

''Yes.''

Lauren turned and paced toward the Christmas tree. Stooping, she stared broodingly at the figurines she'd placed there. When he'd seen the first one, he'd thought perhaps it was part of a crèche scene. In the past day, two more figurines had joined the first, all portraying the same woman in different poses, so his initial guess had been wrong. Alessandro studied them as he waited for Lauren's response. In the original, the woman sat curled up, chin in hand, quiet and peaceful. It was the one he'd initially thought a Madonna figure. In the second she exploded with life, arms flung wide, hair flaring around her, the pose one of ultimate happiness. But in the third she sat quietly again, in repose and notably pregnant.

Meg.

So that's what this was about. Alessandro closed his eyes, struggling to decide how best to handle what had to be said. ''Would she have been upset that we'd developed feelings for each other?'' he finally asked.

Lauren didn't feign confusion. ''No. Believe it or not, she'd have been pleased.''

''Does it bother you that I apparently loved Meg at one time? Or is it fear that keeps you from coming to me?''

She stilled, refusing to look at him. ''Fear?''

''Are you afraid that I'll leave you the way I left

Meg? Are you afraid that my feelings for you might be as fleeting as you think they were for her?''

Lauren rose in a flash, pirouetting to confront him, her towel flaring around her thighs. She didn't back down beneath his steady regard. ''Yes. That's precisely what I think.''

''Was that what your sister told you I'd do? Was she bitter when I didn't return?''

''She wasn't like that!''

''Then tell me how it went down. Tell me what she was like since I can't remember.''

The words ripped loose, months of pent-up anguish. ''She was as glorious at the end, as she was at the beginning. A joyful human being. And I watched her fade before my eyes, inch by agonizing inch. Even those last two months when there was so little left I could lift her in my arms as easily as I could lift Nicky, her spirit persevered. It was a great, sweet, loving spirit.'' Lauren's breath came in harsh sobs. ''She believed the best in people and never gave up hope.''

''Dammit all! What are you trying to tell me?''

''I promised her. I promised her I'd bring Nicky to you. Okay? And I've kept that promise.''

''Is that why you came?'' he demanded in disbelief. ''Because of Meg?''

''*Yes!* It was the last thing in this world she asked me to do. Don't you get it? I'd never have tracked you down, otherwise.''

''And now that you have? What?'' He glared. ''You're planning to leave?''

''You still don't understand. My sister never lost faith in you. *I did.* I'm the one who gave up, who believed you were never coming back. She asked me to phone and I refused. What was the point? I said. You'd gotten what you wanted and slunk off with a happy smile, a cocky walk and nary a look behind. But she made me promise I'd find you. That I'd ask what happened, before condemning you. She told me over and over that you'd never desert... Desert—'' Her throat closed over and she covered her mouth with her hand.

"She was right and you were wrong, is that what you're saying?"

Lauren silently nodded, tears sliding down her cheeks.

"So I forgot the great love of my life, a love that meant everything to her. I allowed her to die unmourned. And you, the only one to mourn her, lost faith. We both let her down, is that it?"

Lauren turned away, crouching like a wounded animal beneath the tree, her face buried in her arms.

He stooped beside her and held her, allowing his touch to say all that he found so difficult to utter. "After you first arrived, you said something that stuck with me."

"I've done nothing but talk since I've arrived and only one thing took?"

A laugh broke free, in some small way managing to ease the pain that scarred them. "I remember a lot of the things you've said. This particular one is appropriate to our current conversation."

"Oh." She sounded somewhat mollified. "In that case, go ahead. What words of wisdom did I slap on you?"

"I was suspicious of your motives in bringing Nick to me." He smiled into her damp hair. "You have to understand, this was back in the days when I doubted he was mine.''

''Fair enough.''

''And you said I wasn't the only one with the right to be suspicious or even cynical. That you had every bit as much right, considering that you had arrived expecting to be recognized. But that you respected me enough to withhold judgment until all the facts were in.''

''But I didn't do that.''

''Sure you did. Maybe not with your sister. But once you were here, you never once accused me of... What did you say? Taking what I wanted and slinking off with a happy smile, a cocky walk and nary a look behind. You were confused, bewildered, hurt. But never hateful or bitter.''

''That doesn't change the fact that I was wrong, Alessandro, and I'm sorry. More sorry than you'll ever know.''

''That makes two of us, sweetheart. Now we have to move past regrets and consider our future. I'm willing to start over, if you are.'' He spooned her against his chest. ''There's only one way I can reassure you that our future will be joined together.''

''And how's that?''

''Time,'' he said simply. ''You have to give us time to build our relationship. Time for the fear to dissipate and for trust to replace it. Time for what we feel for each other to grow and solidify into something that will bind us together for the rest of our lives.''

''And if we don't have that time?''

It wasn't what he'd expected her to say. ''We have all the time you need. You set the pace.''

"Like tonight?"

"If you want to wait, we will." They were probably the hardest words he'd ever uttered.

She didn't say anything for a while. Then slowly, she shifted in his embrace and with a touch so gentle he didn't notice it at first, her hands moved on him. Buttons gave way, one by one, and she pushed his shirt from his shoulders. Snaps and a zip loosened the fit of his jeans before those, too, were stripped away. When the last of his clothing had been removed, she opened her towel. It dropped to the floor behind her and she followed it down, reclining beneath the Christmas tree.

"Are you sure?" he asked.

"Very sure."

Alessandro came to her, kissing a path from the sweetness of her mouth, to the peach-toned peaks of her breasts, to the soft indentation of her belly. She was utterly beautiful, a creature of silver and light, a woman made to be cherished. He tried to tell her how he felt with each lingering touch, explain without words the emotions he'd always kept locked away. Each stroke of his hand became the most beautiful poetry ever written. Each hungry kiss a story of forever-lasting love. And she encouraged him, called to him with her siren's voice, singing a song that reverberated with familiarity. He'd known women before. He'd known completion before.

But not like this. Never like this.

He cupped the back of her knees, caressing upward along the taut skin of her thighs. Her buttocks slipped into his palms, filling them. For such a little thing, there were parts of her that were deliciously full and lush. This was one. She encouraged his efforts with a husky moan, lifting herself toward him, and he slipped into the juncture between her thighs, fitting himself to her. Her legs wrapped around his hips, locking him tight against the true core of her passion.

With a soft cry of pleasure, she reached for him, framing his face, her touch quieting the pain that had haunted him for months. In that timeless moment, she was open to him and he saw clear to her soul. There was pain and sorrow, regrets and shattered dreams. But there was also hope. And there was a love so deep and profound, it couldn't be mistaken for anything else.

The need to possess grew stronger and he sculpted her body, drawing delicate images across her skin until she vibrated with hunger. She was all lean tension, her muscles clenching with the slow escalation of her passion. He brushed his hands across the sensitive skin of her belly and then lower. She shivered in his arms, calling again in her siren's voice.

He drove home, joining them. "Do you still doubt we were meant for each other?" he demanded. "See how perfectly we fit together? This is our future. No matter how hard we fight it, it won't be denied."

"Are you sure, Alessandro?" She repeated his own words back to him.

"I believe it with a heart I didn't think I possessed and a soul you brought to life."

Her eyes burned with the depths of her love. "I want a future with you."

"You have one. You'll always have one."

The need for words vanished and desire took over. And then something more than desire. With their joining came a connection. A completion. A unity that mated them for all time. It was Christmas. A time for miracles. In their love, they found one. Alessandro's last coherent thought was that there were unicorns and Santa Claus and impossible dreams abroad in his world.

They'd been born again in the soft blue eyes of a woman who'd claimed to lack faith while bringing to life the miracle she'd promised.

CHAPTER NINE

Christmas morning…

SHE came to him again, all silk and sweetness and heady feminine perfume. This time, something felt different about their relationship, out of kilter. Alessandro scowled. He'd hurt her. He hadn't meant to. But he'd managed it, anyway, and he was furious with himself for handling their parting so awkwardly. With the exception of Rocco, any one of his other brothers would have known the right words to use. Charm came naturally to them.

They stood beneath the same ancient oak where they'd celebrated spring's arrival by making love. Over the past few days, the massive branches had exploded in a flurry of newborn leaves. Twilight was fast approaching and shadows crept from the surrounding woods. She wouldn't look at him, but stared instead at the purple crocuses clinging to the base of the tree. No doubt she was trying to hide her tears.

"You know I don't want to leave," he began.

"I have to go, Alessandro," Lauren whispered into his dream.

"But you don't have any choice." Meg's hair concealed her expression, falling across her cheek in a pale blond swathe. "I understand that."

"Are you sure you won't come with me?" It was at least the tenth time he'd asked.

She shook her head. "I can't go any more than you can stay."

"I have a present for you. And for Nicky, too. I'll put it beneath the tree before I go. Luc promised to pass on my message. I just hope he gets it straight. He isn't very good at memorizing, is he? He kept saying it was because I'd called so late, but I think that's an excuse." She took a deep breath before continuing. "And the twins will see that I get safely to the airport. They should be here in a few more hours."

"It's Lauren, isn't it?"

"I'm just not willing to leave right now," she maintained with a familiar hint of stubbornness.

"I understand." And he did. Families stuck together, bound by responsibility and duty, but most of all by love. "We won't be apart for long," he consoled. "Only for a couple of weeks. A month at most. If I could hand these meetings off to anyone else, I would."

"I haven't told you everything I should have. And…and I have loose ends to tie up at home. I got myself in a bit of a fix before I left. It's time to go back and straighten out the whole mess. To do what's right. You'll watch over Nicky, won't you? You'll love him with all your heart just like I do."

"I know you don't want to leave. I also know you have to do what's right." She turned then and threw herself into his arms. "Oh, Alessandro. I love you. I wish you wouldn't leave."

"I love you, Alessandro. You may not understand how that's possible. But I do."

She was killing him, inch by gut-wrenching inch.

"I love you, too," he told her, his voice rough with emotion. *"Don't you ever forget that."*

"Never. I promise."

"When I come back—if you let me come back…"
He was helpless to resist.

"I'll explain everything."
He wanted her.

"And if you're willing to let me stay…" Her voice broke, tears slipping down her cheeks. "If you'll—"
Needed her.

"If you'll still allow me in your life and Nicky's…"

"Meg?" Alessandro thrust the dream away, gripped by an urgency he couldn't explain. "Lauren? Honey?" She wasn't in his arms anymore and he sat up in alarm, terrified that he'd somehow lost her.

"I'm here." She brushed a hand across her face before moving from her stance beside the Christmas tree. A waning moon caught her in its gentle glow, dusting her with silver starlight. At some point, she'd put on her night shift and it floated around her in a transparent wisp, her nudity silhouetted against the stark white cotton. "I'm sorry to wake you."

He fought the remnants of the dream, troubled that Meg continued to hold center stage in them when it was Lauren he wanted. Why did the memories keep haunting him? It was almost as if he'd forgotten something, something he urgently needed to remember. "What time is it?"

"Just before midnight."

"Midnight?" His scrutiny sharpened. "What's wrong? What are you doing up?"

She shrugged, drifting close enough for him to see

the telltale sheen of moisture on her cheeks. ''Nothing's wrong. I had Christmas preparations to finish before morning.''

The suspicion that something was out of kilter grew stronger. ''We're a pathetic pair, you know that?'' he pretended to grouse. ''We should have been able to sleep through the night just this once. After all, it's Christmas and all good boys and girls should be in bed.'' He flashed her a wicked grin. ''Preferably together.''

To his relief, she responded with an answering smile. ''You and I did bed down together. We even shared a peaceful sleep.'' Her smile turned wry. ''For a while, anyway.''

''Until you left.''

''What's going on, Alessandro? Wait. I think I can guess.'' Lauren knelt beside him and touched his shoulder, urging him backward into the thick carpet. ''You had another of your dreams, didn't you?''

Damn. There were times she proved distressingly perceptive. Evasion seemed the sensible course of action. He was too tired to try anything else. ''Your hands are like ice. Come here and let me warm you.''

He tugged at her arm, sending her sprawling across him. Then he wrapped himself around her, allowing his heat to drive the chill from her body. Even holding her this close, images from the dream wouldn't go away. Something about a tree. And purple crocuses. He'd said something. Something wrong. But exhaustion kept him from remembering what.

''I'm not ready to go back to sleep, Alessandro,'' Lauren protested, even as she curled up against him. ''I still have a few last chores to take care of.''

''The chores can wait. Leave the rest for tonight.

Anything else you want to fix up, can be done after breakfast. Nick won't mind, and neither will I. In fact, we'll both pitch in and help.''

"It won't take me long. I can get everything done real quick while you sleep.''

"I'm not sure I can sleep. Not without you.'' He couldn't see her expression and it bothered him. But he didn't dare allow her to escape again. He knew with an absolute certainty that if she left his embrace, she wouldn't come back. ''Would you rather we go to my bedroom? The mattress would be a hell of a lot more comfortable than the floor.''

"Not yet. It's…it's almost Christmas. I'd like to welcome it here beneath the tree with you. It'll be a special memory.''

It was a small thing to ask. ''Okay. If that's what you want.'' Anything to keep her nearby. Another thought struck him. ''Were you talking to me before I woke? I could have sworn I heard your voice.''

"Yes.'' It was her turn to sound evasive.

"What did you say?''

"It's nothing important.'' Her hands were gentle on him. Loving. Reassuring. ''It'll keep until morning.''

He pillowed her head with his shoulder and kept his arms tight around her. She wouldn't escape again. Not without him realizing it. He released his breath in a slow sigh. Everything would work out. They just needed time.

And they had plenty of that.

Then he slept, as did the woman in his arms. Peacefully, even dreamlessly, cocooned within each other's embrace.

*   *   *

Alessandro didn't know how much later he awoke. It was after midnight, but long before dawn. Above him the tree signified the arrival of Christmas, its boughs holding the outward expression of all their joy, while beneath the tree lay their fears—symbolized by the three very different faces of the woman whose ghost stood between them.

He knew his feelings for Meg must have been intense, the dreams told him that much. But he couldn't remember enough of the specifics or the full scope of his emotions at that time, to completely grasp the love he'd experienced or the loss of that love. Nor could his emotions have been as deep and everlasting as what he now felt for the woman in his arms. It wasn't possible.

He gazed at the figurines placed so lovingly beneath the tree and a profound sadness gripped him. So many regrets. A life cut far too short. A love that had never had a chance to ripen. A child who'd never know his true mother. But if even a tenth of the characteristics Lauren had used to describe her sister were true, Meg wouldn't object to his having found love again. Not when her last wish had been one of such unstinting generosity.

Not when she'd chosen as her final act to gift him with their baby.

He brushed a fingertip over each of Lauren's creations, one after another. ''You understand, don't you? Maybe you even hoped it would happen.'' The three figurines remained frozen in their predetermined positions—contemplative, joyful, and quietly accepting. Alessandro knew the moment of decision had come. What had baseball great Yogi Berra always said? When you reach a fork in the road, take it?

Something like that. Well, he'd reached that fork and he was taking it because they both led to the same place—a life and home with the two people he loved most in the world.

Lauren stirred beside him. "Why are you frowning?" she asked, her voice sleep-husked.

He smiled tenderly. "Did my frowning wake you?"

"Yup." She rubbed rumpled silvery layers from her face. "I heard it clear as anything, right dab-smack in the middle of my dream."

"My frown's gone now. And it won't be back anytime soon."

"Promise?" Her voice faded as sleep reclaimed her.

"I promise, love." He glanced at the figurines. It was time to put the ghosts of his former relationship to rest and move on. "Goodbye, Meg," he whispered. Lifting Lauren in his arms, he walked away.

He didn't look back.

"Lauren?" Alessandro bolted upright in bed. The space beside him felt empty and cold and the sun had crept high enough to warn that daybreak had come and gone several hours ago. "No. Aw, hell. No, no, no. I called her Meg. I did. I just know I did." He scrubbed his hands across his face. It had been when he'd first woken up from that damned dream, the one he'd been so certain would never haunt him again. "This can't be good."

On the nightstand table beside him sat the flowerpot of crocuses he'd given Lauren. They were blooming. He stared at the flowers for a full minute before comprehension crashed down on him. She'd left them as a farewell gift. Little purple cups, empty of hope, came the errant thought. He shook his head, refusing to acknowledge the inescapable truth. No, dammit! Lauren hadn't left. He couldn't bear losing her, anymore than he could stand to lose—

Nicky!

He exploded from beneath the covers and raced across the hallway to his son's room. The crib was empty. He swore, the Italian as passionate as it was ear-blistering.

"Shame on you, little brother. You should know better than to use that sort of language in front of an impressionable child."

Alessandro spun around to confront Luc. His relief at seeing Nick in his brother's arms was so profound, it took him a full minute to summon up a greeting. "What the hell are you doing here?"

"Language," Luc repeated in disgust. "If you're going to reproduce, you'll have to learn to clean up your act so your little reproductions don't follow the bad example you set."

"Where's—"

"Gone." Luc inclined his head toward the living area. "She left a note and some gifts under the tree. There's one for you and one for this little guy. Merry Christmas, by the way."

Alessandro held out his arms to Nick. His son practically flung himself from Luc's grasp. "Let's see what your momma left us," he said grimly enough that Nick's little face puckered.

"Did I mention that kids are also sensitive to the mood of their parents?"

Alessandro brushed past his brother and headed for

the living room. "So you've decided he's mine, have you?"

"He's the spitting image of you. I'd say congratulations were in order."

"Thanks. You still haven't explained what you're doing here."

"Didn't I mention? The whole family's coming to celebrate Christmas with you. It was Lauren's idea. She called and said you'd be needy, or words to that effect."

"I don't have time to entertain. I have a missing woman to track down."

"I suggest you open your presents first." When Alessandro opened his mouth to argue, Luc added, "It was Lauren's last request before she left."

Alessandro hesitated by the Christmas tree. She'd added to the figurines of the woman. There were now five in all. Beside them were two boxes, one large and one small. The large one was addressed to Nick. It had been neatly wrapped with handmade paper, a small grinning stick elf taking the place of a bow. Setting Nick on the floor, Alessandro opened it. It contained a quilt, one that must have taken months and months of work to complete, the predominate colors silver and baby blue.

"Look at this, Nick," he murmured. "I don't think I've ever seen anything so beautiful. Have you?"

Each square of the quilt contained an appliquéd scene. The scenes followed a time line, starting with an eerily familiar moment in a restaurant. His gaze shifted from one square to the next. There was the picnic in the woods. And in another a snowcapped purple crocus. Another must have been from the days of Meg's pregnancy. Still another, the birth of Nick.

Square after square chronicled his courtship of Meg and the birth of their son.

Without a word, he reached for the second box and ripped it open, gently tipping the contents into the palm of his hand. Out tumbled the chain Dom had given him the day his mother had been buried, along with her wedding band. He closed his eyes, allowing the grief to wash over him.

"I have to go. I have to find her."

"She flew back to North Carolina."

"How do you know?" Alessandro turned his head to stare at his brother, the last vestiges of his control vanishing. *"How the hell do you know?"*

"Because I had Marco and Stefano drive her to the airport. She called sometime around midnight and begged us to come and get her." He shrugged. "What were we supposed to do?"

"What were you…?" Alessandro lunged at his brother, wrapping a fist around Luc's shirt collar, his Italian coming fast and furious. "You should have told her no. You should have told her *hell* no. And now you'd better come up with a damned good explanation for why you didn't. Let me warn you, if it's not one I like, I'll tear you apart."

"She had to attend a child welfare hearing. They were deciding whether or not to take Nick away from her. She offered her car in exchange for an airplane ticket. The crazy woman even signed over the pink slip."

Alessandro's teeth came together with a snap. "What are you talking about?"

"Her car. Did she tell you she calls it Babe?" Luc tilted his head to a contemplative angle. "I'm not sure

Grace would approve of my owning a car named Babe.''

"*Cretino!* Not the car. What child welfare hearing? Why would anyone try to take Nick from her?''

Luc shrugged. ''How should I know? I'm just repeating what she told me. If you want the rest of the story, you'll have to get it from her.''

''That might be a little difficult since *she's not here to ask!*'' His fury had no affect on his brother whatsoever.

''As for the twins driving her to the airport,'' Luc continued with impressive calm, ''I had them take her because I figured if anyone had a shot at charming her out of leaving, they would. They called an hour ago.''

''And?''

''It would seem she never stopped crying the entire time they were with her. She soaked Marco's shirt on the drive to the airport and wept all over Stefano while they checked in.'' He hesitated. ''I'm sorry, Alessandro. It would seem the Salvatore charm leaves something to be desired. She got on the plane, sobbing every step of the way, but she did get on.''

''She left?''

''Yeah. She left.'' Luc stared pointedly at Alessandro's hand. ''You want to let go now?''

''No. I'd like to beat you to a bloody pulp.'' He released his brother. ''So what now? How do I find her?''

''She gave me a message for you.''

His anger flared again, hotter than before. ''ou going to give it to me or is this one more thing I've to beat out of you?''

Luc held up his hands. ''No need to i

don't think I can get her accent quite right, but she said something along the lines of, don't forget to be quiet and look. That everything is whispering, trying to tell you their special secrets. She made me repeat it three times before she was satisfied I had it straight. Maybe if it hadn't been so late, I wouldn't have had so much trouble.''

Alessandro froze. He knew those words. He'd heard them once upon a time in a cabin filled with "critters." "Is that all she said?"

"Not quite. She also said to remind you that home is where the heart is."

Be quiet and look. Home is where the heart is.

His gaze fell on the figurines beneath the Christmas tree and he studied them again. The first three hadn't changed. Meg still sat in peaceful repose in the first, dancing with explosive joy in the second and remained serenely pregnant in the third. He switched his attention to the additions.

Next came the birth of their child. It was another happy scene, the baby held aloft, Meg's hair floating long and free. But in the last her shorn head was tipped backward, her posture one of profound grief. Was this when she'd discovered she was dying? he wondered uneasily. He forced himself to study the last figure, suddenly noticing she held something clutched in her arms. At first he thought it was the baby. And then, after looking closer, he realized it was another woman.

For a long time he could only stare.

"Dio!" Comprehension crashed over him. He snatched up the quilt and went through it again panel by panel. *Everything around here is whispering to you, trying to tell you their special secrets.* He un-

derstood now. "The pink slip. Quick. Give me the pink slip."

"What? Oh, right. Sure." Luc thrust his hand in his pocket and pulled out the crumpled vehicle title. "Here."

It took Alessandro two seconds to find what he was looking for. "I'm leaving," he informed Luc. "I have to find her. Now."

"Because of a stupid pink slip?" Luc shook his head. "It's Christmas. The family's coming. You're needy, remember? You can't just leave."

"Watch me." He'd been promised a Christmas miracle and, by heaven, he'd gotten one. Too bad that miracle had walked out the door and climbed on an eastbound plane before he'd had a chance to explain it to her. Didn't she understand?

She was his miracle.

"Where are you going?" Luc grimaced. "As if I didn't know."

"I'm going to find my wife and bring her home." Alessandro snatched up his son and cradled him close. "Assuming I can find her."

Luc's jaw dropped "Your *wife?*"

"I'll explain later."

CHAPTER TEN

The days following Christmas…

SHE came to him again, all silk and sweetness and heady feminine perfume. They were back beneath the ancient oak, where it had all ended. Back where the beauty of spring came in new-leaf green and purple cups of hope. Back where the woman in his arms shed tears of farewell.

"Meg? Honey?"

She still wouldn't look at him, but he could feel a suspicious moisture dampening his shirt. He couldn't count how many shirts she'd leaked over in the time they'd been together. She had to be the "cryingest" woman he'd ever met. Not that she'd ever used her tears as leverage. Hell, no. They were just a natural part of her personality.

"I'm sorry, Alessandro." Yup. Definitely tears. "I don't mean to make this any more difficult than it is. It's just… Your flight doesn't leave until tomorrow morning."

"Six a.m."

"Can't we have tonight together?"

It wouldn't be enough. Nothing would satisfy him until the day he put a ring— He swore beneath his breath. What an idiot he'd been. Why hadn't he thought of this before? "Let's get married." He couldn't say where the words had come from, but they felt right. Necessary. Inevitable. "Let's get married now."

Tension raced through her. "Married?"

"Well, what the hell do you think I've been talking about these past several days?"

"I thought after Rhonda—"

"You and Rhonda are nothing alike and never could be." He shook his head in disgust. "I don't know why I didn't think of this sooner. Maybe if I had we could have put together a proper ceremony before I left for San Francisco. But it's too late now. The county offices are closed."

"I don't understand."

He reached around his neck and removed the chain. Opening the clasp he freed his mother's ring. "Give me your hand."

Meg took a step backward, staring in confusion. "Just what in the blue blazes are you up to?"

"Do it. Give me your left hand." ·

The instant she complied, he slipped the ring on the fourth finger. He didn't give her a chance to protest, but started speaking. "I, Alessandro Vittorio Salvatore, take thee, Margaret Mary Williams, to be my lawfully wedded wife."

"What are you doing, you crazy man?"

His jaw acquired a stubborn slant. "I'm marrying you. It may not be legally binding, but it joins us as far as I'm concerned. Now where was I? Oh, right. To love, honor and cherish until death do us part." For the first time, he felt a faint hesitancy. "It's your turn—assuming you want to marry me."

"Of course I want to marry you. How can you doubt it?"

Taking a deep breath, she repeated the vows in a

voice at one with the mountains surrounding them. The minute she finished, he sealed their promise with a desperate kiss. The hell with it. He would stay, even though it meant leaving her bed long before daybreak in order to make his flight. If it gave them another few hours together, it would be worth it.

"As far as I'm concerned, you're my wife. You got that?" he demanded fiercely. "I'm not even going to say goodbye. Because this isn't a goodbye."

A gentle breeze washed over them and the setting sun broke through the rich verdant canopy of the ancient oak, encircling them in its waning rays of light and warmth. Meg flung her arms wide in sheer joy and spun in a circle. Her hair spread around in a flowing, silken cape, the silvery highlights glittering like fairy dust. Dizzy, she tumbled into Alessandro's arms. And finally she looked at him.

"My husband," she whispered, her soft, powder-blue eyes brilliant with passion. "How I love you."

He was helpless to resist. He wanted her. Needed her.

He left her.

The following week was the most frustrating of Alessandro's life. He'd never realized how big Asheville was, or how many mountains surrounded it. Or how difficult it would be to find a woman who didn't want to be found. Even attempting to hire a private investigator had proven fruitless. It was the holidays and quite a few businesses had closed for the week. Those few who answered the phone, didn't have time to take on the job.

Strangely, the dreams had stopped. But he suspected that was because he understood them now, that he'd figured out what had happened during those missing two weeks and what he was supposed to remember. And still he searched, refusing to give up. Unable to give up.

His luck finally changed on New Year's Eve.

He'd taken to driving aimlessly around the outskirts of Asheville whenever he felt particularly dispirited. Nick, strapped into a car seat in the back, made life easier by considering the rides a treat. Cruising along a small back road, Alessandro continued a full mile past the restaurant before the name clicked in his head.

LuLu's.

Pulling the car to the side of the road, he made a cautious U-turn and returned to the diner. A Closed sign sat askew in the window. But he knew the place, could see brief flashes of images. Meg pausing by his table, a sassy grin on her face. Meg chatting with the regulars and asking after their families. Meg, her face sheet-white, begging for a ride to the hospital, her sister clutched in her arms.

"We found her, little buddy," he whispered to Nick. "We found your momma."

"Ma-ma," he repeated, tears welling up in his eyes.

"Not long now. I promise. Momma will be home soon."

Now all he had to do was utilize a bit of logic and reason. First, he'd try and find the owner of the diner and ask for directions to the Williams's place. Or if that didn't work, he'd explore each road from here outward, progressing in a methodical search pattern. Or... He closed his eyes. Or he could go with his gut instincts, something he couldn't ever remember attempting before.

He didn't hesitate. Putting the car in gear, he exited the parking lot and started driving. Until that moment he'd never realized how difficult it was to *not* think. He had to pull over several times and clear his mind. Trying to force the memories flat-out didn't work. In the end, he made three wrong turns. But the instant he saw the little dirt road darting off the main drag, he knew he'd done it. He didn't even need the white sign that read ''Williams''—a sign held by a combative family of stick elves—to tell him he'd found his way back home.

He eased along the winding drive, not rushing anymore. With every twist and dip more and more memories returned. Long walks through the forest. The picnic. The snowstorm that had stranded him at the cabin with Meg, while Lauren had been forced to stay with a friend in Asheville. Making love in front of the fireplace.

The woods surrounding the cabin were alive with stick figures of all sizes. Herds of deer peeked from behind bushes, creative birdhouses that looked like the birds they'd been designed to house clung to tree trunks, trolls and elves and dragons, skunks and raccoons and 'possum cavorted on top of fallen logs, in the crooks of trees, and along every ridge and hollow. He knew from having methodically counted his way through the woods that the ''critters'' numbered in the hundreds.

Pulling up to the front door of the cabin, he stared across the mountaintop. The trees were naked without their springtime apparel and he could just make out the ancient oak on the next hillside, its barren branches flung wide like a woman awaiting her absent lover's embrace. That's where he and Meg had consummated their relationship on the first day of spring, the place his son had been conceived. And that's where he and Meg had made the vows that bound them still. It was also where, he was willing to bet, he'd find a lovingly tended grave site. It would be adorned with masses of sleeping purple crocuses, the petite flowers awaiting spring's rebirth to lift their cups of hope heavenward in prayerful supplication.

He turned toward Nick, shaking his head when he realized his son had fallen sound asleep. Perhaps it was for the best. This would give him an opportunity to talk to his ''wife'' in private. Gently, he unstrapped the carrier and lifted it, baby and all, from the car. He didn't bother to knock on the cabin door, but walked right in. At first he didn't think anyone was home. But then a small movement by the fireplace drew his gaze.

''Hello, Meg,'' he said simply.

For a minute he didn't think she'd answer. ''Hello, Alessandro.'' Her prosaic reply sounded tired. Dispirited. ''I assume you figured it out?''

''It took a while, but the message you left with Luc helped. Once I was quiet enough, I found your special secrets. They came as quite a surprise.'' A gross understatement, if he'd ever heard one.

''I wondered whether or not you'd come once you learned the truth.''

''More doubts?''

She remained cloaked in gloom but he could just make out the flash of silver as she nodded. ''Guess I'll need to work harder on breaking that habit.''

''Yes, you will.'' He set the car seat on the floor.

"Aren't you going to say hello to your son?" he asked, knowing the question would drive her from the shadows. Sure enough she darted forward, hesitating at the last minute when she saw Nick sleeping.

"How is he?"

"He misses you. Hell, sweetheart. I miss you, too." Still she hesitated and he spread his arms wide. It was all the encouragement she needed. She flung herself into his embrace and burst into tears. "You are the cryingest woman I ever did meet," he whispered against the top of her head. He wrapped her up in a bone-crunching hug. "And if you ever pull another stunt like this, you and I will be having a serious difference of opinion."

"I'm sorry, Alessandro," she managed between sobs. "I'm sorry I lied to you. I'm sorry I left."

"Shh. I'm not angry. Confused. Worried. A bit hurt. But not angry."

"I thought you'd be nail-bitin' furious."

"Well…" He shrugged. "I might have been somewhat peeved when I first discovered you'd taken off."

"I didn't have any choice. I had to tell child welfare about Nick. And… And I had to give you time to make a decision about us."

"There's never been any question about us, though I have one or two about child welfare." He ran his fingers through her shorn locks. "Then there's the question of why you cut your hair. And why you used your sister's name instead of telling me who you were from the start. And then there's the small issue of Nick and his conception."

"Have you gotten the results of the paternity test, yet?"

"Probably. Or I would have if I'd been home.

Instead I've been wandering around Asheville for a week trying to find a wife who's gone missing.''

She pulled away, not that he let her go far. It would be a long time before he felt comfortable having her out of arm's reach. "Then you don't know for sure Nick's your son.''

"Oh, I know he's mine. I seem to recall our making love once or—''

"Your memory?'' she interrupted eagerly. "It's come back?''

"Bits and pieces. Flashes. Dreams.'' He gathered her close again. "I doubt I'll ever remember everything. But I'll have you to fill in the gaps.''

She immediately looked away, fighting to control the slight quiver of her chin. He could guess what had upset her. She was afraid that once he knew all her secrets, he wouldn't want her anymore, that he'd turn on her. Maybe if he hadn't deserted her or if she hadn't lost faith in him as a result, she'd have been spared some of her current torment. But then, after what she'd gone through in the past year and a half, it was a wonder she remained so loving and generous. A lesser woman would have become embittered.

He swept a hand down her spine and up her arms before forking his fingers deep into her hair. He couldn't restrain the urge to touch her, to reassure himself that he'd actually found her and held her safe within his arms. "What I've never understood is how Nick was conceived.''

She flashed him a speaking glance. "The usual way tends to get the job done.''

He chuckled. "Cute. What I mean is, what happened to the birth control? I'm usually a fanatic about it.''

To his private amusement a hint of a blush tinted her cheeks. He'd never known a woman who could go from earthy to shy over so little provocation. "It was when we made love in the woods."

"The first day of spring?"

"Yes."

"We forgot to pack the picnic basket with all the bare essentials?" he inquired with impressive diplomacy.

"Bingo." She held up a hand. "But all was not lost, or so you thought. You had your wallet with you."

He looked blank for a moment. "Oh, right. I forgot my wallet came fully equipped."

"Yes, well... Apparently the equipment in question had been in there since that oak we were dining under was a mere acorn."

"Didn't hold up to minimum acceptable standards?"

"It split cleaner than an overstuffed sausage," came her succinct reply.

He winced. "Your imagery leaves something to be desired."

Her scrutiny turned unexpectedly intense. "Do you recall your reaction at the time?"

"No. But I can guess."

"I don't think you can."

"I'd have apologized with great charm." He offered a teasing grin. "A Salvatore characteristic, you understand, even if I'm not as slick as some of my brothers."

She didn't respond to his humor. He could feel her tension and wondered at the cause. "And then?"

Meg didn't deserve anything less than absolute

honesty. "And then I imagine I'd have reacted the same way I did Christmas Eve when I realized we'd screwed up on the birth control. I'd have been quietly pleased."

She stared in wonder, her tension dissipating. "How did you know?"

"Because it would have forced the issue between us. I'd just come off a divorce and I suspect you were reluctant to make a commitment, worried that my feelings for you were transient." He shrugged. "It was a reasonable assumption given the circumstances."

"Reasonable for someone who lacked faith."

"Stop it, Meg." He tilted her face to his. "We all have our failings. It's what makes us human. What's happened between us will also strengthen our commitment. Neither of us will doubt the other again, will we?"

"Not a chance." She caught her lip between her teeth. "We did mess up on the birth control last week, didn't we?"

"Do you mind?"

She shook her head. "No. I'd prefer waiting a bit before having another baby. But, no."

That was all he needed to hear. "Now tell me the rest. Why the hell did you cut your hair?"

It was the wrong question to ask. She burst into tears. Picking her up, he carried her to a nearby chair, one of the few sticks of furniture remaining in the cabin. Settling her on his lap, he held her until she'd cried herself out. Or cried herself out for the next few minutes.

"I gave my hair to Lauren."

Aw, hell. "Tell me about it."

"My sister cut her hair before she started radiation treatment. It would have fallen out, anyway, she told me, so why not save what she could? I thought she'd make it into a wig. Instead she donated every last strand to a charity for children with cancer."

"I gather when you discovered what she'd done, you cut yours and gave it to her as a gift?"

"Yes."

He couldn't speak for a full minute. "I'm so sorry."

"Do you remember her, Alessandro?" Meg dropped her head to his shoulder. "Do you remember her sweetness? Her laughter? Her generosity? She was such a special person. And she never gave up hope that you and I would find each other again. If she hadn't made me promise, I probably wouldn't have gone looking for you. After all, my phone calls had never been returned, so I assumed your feelings for me had changed. Why should I hunt you down? It was clear you didn't want me anymore. I'd lost every bit of faith. But Lauren hadn't. Not once. Not ever."

"We owe her a lot, don't we?"

"It was her last gift to us."

Silence reigned. "What happened after Lauren died?" Alessandro eventually asked. "I gather that's when child welfare got involved."

The breath shuddered in Meg's lungs. "You know about that, too?"

"I'd like to hear your version."

"It was the same as Christmas Eve at your cabin." She curled into him, clinging. "I'd fallen asleep and Nick tried to pull himself up using the tablecloth. Everything came crashing down on him. Oh,

Alessandro. I was so scared. There were dishes and glasses. There was even a knife. He could have been killed.''

''Instead he was bruised.''

''And cut. One of the glasses got him.'' She shuddered. ''I was terrified. I grabbed him, ran for the car and drove as fast as I could to the hospital.''

''And when they asked what had happened, you told them.''

She nodded. ''The doctor believed I'd been negligent because I'd been sleeping when I should have been tending to him. He reported the incident to the child welfare people. When I found out what he'd done I panicked. I bundled Nick up, loaded Babe with as many of our possessions as would fit and lit out of there. I knew if I could just get to you, you'd take our son and keep him safe.''

''You knew that?'' he asked in a rough voice. ''Even after you hadn't heard from me in close to two years, you were sure enough of my reaction to work your way across country to find me?''

''Yes.'' Her answer was simple, absolute and utterly sincere. ''If there was one thing I did have faith in, it was your feelings toward family. The Salvatores may have charm, but more than that they have a deep and abiding love for family. I knew you'd care for Nick and make sure no further harm came to him. Besides, I'd promised Lauren.''

''Weren't you afraid I'd take him away from you?''

A tiny tremor shot through her, confirming his guess. ''I didn't know what would happen or how you'd react. But even if you were granted legal custody, at least Nick would be with his daddy instead of in a foster home. I couldn't risk losing him to social services, Alessandro. Not after what you'd been through as a child. You'd never have forgiven me.''

''Speaking of social services, why the hell didn't you tell them about Lauren? Why didn't you explain how you'd spent the last several months nursing your dying sister while caring for a baby?''

''Do you think it would have made a difference?''

''Would it…?'' He thrust a hand through his hair. ''Yeah. It would have made a difference. The government doesn't want to take babies away from their mothers, sweetheart. Not without just cause. They much prefer finding ways to help. When I described the circumstances to the social worker, she was shocked. They had no idea what you'd been through.''

''You spoke to the people at child welfare?''

''The minute I hit town. I was trying to find you.''

''Didn't they give you my address?''

''A small matter of red tape. We're not married, remember?''

For some reason that amused her. ''I assume your Salvatore charm has its limitations?''

''Maybe if I'd thought to bring Marco or Stefano or Luc with me,'' he confessed with appropriate humility. ''Luc in particular has a way with social workers.''

''I could have used his help, too. They were furious with me when I met with them this past week.''

''Something to do with your folding your arms across your chest and refusing to give them any information about yourself other than your name and social security number?'' His brows pulled together in a frown. "Maybe that's why I couldn't wheedle an address out of them. They probably didn't have it."

She winced. "I suppose that might have been part of the problem. My attitude did seem to annoy them a tad. I did give them everything they needed to know about you so they could satisfy themselves that Nick was in good hands."

"In that case, you'll be pleased to learn that I explained the events of the past year and the matter is officially closed."

Relief lightened her expression. "Really?"

"Really. Which brings us to the most crucial question of all."

"Why didn't I tell you I was Nick's momma right from the start?"

"Yes." Regret underscored his words. "It was because I didn't recognize you, wasn't it?"

"For the most part." She caught her lower lip between her teeth. "It hurt to think that the time we'd spent together meant so little that you didn't remember it. Or me. But I figured establishing Nicky's paternity was the most crucial issue, not my hurt pride, so I decided to play the part of his aunt instead of his momma. If I'd told you we'd been lovers then we'd have been dealing with our past relationship instead of with what was best for our son."

"On top of which, you were exhausted."

She didn't deny it. "I couldn't handle any more emotional upsets. I had the energy to fight for Nick—"

"But not for yourself?"

"No," she admitted.

"Dammit, Meg. What I don't understand is why you left."

Her hands fisted in his shirt. "It was the hardest thing I've ever done. After we made love, I had to get away. I'd done exactly what I'd sworn I wouldn't."

"Fallen in love again?"

She bowed her head. "Yes."

"Didn't it occur to you that I'd fallen in love, as well?" A hint of an accent betrayed the depth of his emotions. "Don't you understand, *bella mia?* What we have is eternal, enduring. Even when I didn't remember falling in love with you that March, even when every bit of logic and reason told me I was making a mistake because it was your sister I must love and that my feelings for you were a reflection of what I felt for her, I still couldn't resist you. Doesn't that tell you anything?"

"It took me a while longer than you to reach that same conclusion. All I knew was that I'd lied to you and when you found out who I really was and how I'd put Nick in harm's way, it would kill your feelings for me. And then there was the cabin." She glanced around, a hint of sadness darkening her expression. "There were loose ends I had to tie up here."

"What sort of loose ends?"

"Half of it belonged to Lauren. She died owing a stack of medical bills."

Alessandro winced. "The bill collectors are forcing a sale?"

"Yes." She shrugged. "It doesn't come as a surprise. I knew before I left that it was only a matter of time before they took it away from me."

"What about all your critters?"

"I'll bring the ones I can and leave the rest. Someone else will have the joy of them."

He let it go for now. Next week, he'd make a few phone calls. Removing the chain from around his neck, he freed his mother's ring. "I've always wondered why I never offered this to Rhonda. After I met you I understood. Deep down I knew she wasn't the woman destined to wear it." He slid the band onto Meg's finger. "I gave this to you once before. This time I'm hoping it'll find a permanent home. Will you marry me, Meg? For real?"

She smiled tremulously. "Beneath an oak tree on a balmy spring day?"

"Not a chance. This is New Year's Eve and as I recall, North Carolina doesn't have a waiting period. What do you say to starting this next year off the right way? The only way. With you as my wife."

She flung her arms around him, smothering his face with kisses. "Yes, yes, *yes!* I'll marry you. Today, if it's possible."

He pulled back, frowning. "What? No tears?"

"Why in the world would I cry?" she asked in utter bewilderment. "I'm happy not sad."

"I haven't noticed that minor detail stopping you before." He smiled in sheer contentment. "You have to be the cryingest woman I've ever known."

"Don't be ridiculous, Alessandro," she retorted, wiping her cheeks. "If there's one thing you can count on, it's that I never cry."

EPILOGUE

The first day of spring…

"I'M NOT sure I want to come here," Meg fussed. "It will make me too sad."

"It won't make you sad. You'll be happy to see the old place."

"No, I think I'll be sad." She slanted him a quick, warning look. "It may even make me cry."

"I don't doubt that for a minute."

Alessandro pulled up outside the Williams's cabin and breathed a sigh of relief. So far, so good. In the months since he'd saved the place from the auction block, it had been a hive of activity, though keeping Meg blissfully unaware of that fact had proven something of a challenge, particularly considering the number of long-distance phone calls she'd intercepted from various contractors.

All in all, they'd done an excellent job, replacing the roof, restaining the shake siding, as well as updating the electrical and plumbing. The work had given the cabin a much-needed facelift without destroying the rustic charm. From where he sat, he could see the addition they'd made to the bathroom, expanding it to include a whirlpool tub. He couldn't wait to see Meg's face when she discovered it.

And then there was one final surprise he'd planned for his wife. A small one. One he hoped she'd like.

Spending each spring at the cabin would be the start of a new tradition, he decided, one he and Meg would continue for the rest of their lives. She emerged from the back of the car having freed Nick from his car seat, her silver-blond hair attractively rumpled. It was a bit longer now, drifting in silky layers over her ears.

"Do you think the owners will mind if we just drop in out of the blue?" she asked nervously.

He emerged from the car and joined her. "They won't mind in the least."

"I don't know how you can say that."

"I can say it because of this." He dangled a set of keys in front of her nose. "Consider it a belated wedding gift."

It took a minute for her to understand. And then it took her three starts to get the question out. "You bought the cabin?" Her voice broke on the last word. "For me?"

He cupped her hand and placed the keys safe and secure in the hollow of her palm. So much of his life resided there, held safely within her tender hold. "For us, my love. For our children and our grandchildren." He tucked a lock of hair behind her ear. "It's important that they're familiar with their roots, don't you think?"

Her powder-blue eyes glittered with tears and a tremulous smile spread across her face. Before she could say anything, he turned her toward the cabin and gave her a gentle nudge. He waited for her to spot the change, waited with keen anticipation for her reaction.

And then she saw it.

Spread in a dense carpet as far as the eye could see

were thousands of purple crocuses, all blooming as though in anticipation of Meg's arrival. It was a fitting tribute to Lauren, he decided, quietly satisfied. If it hadn't been for the promise she'd extracted, he might never have known his current joy. Slowly, Meg set Nick on the ground and for a minute he thought her knees would buckle. He started for her at the same instant she whirled to face him. Then she was running, leaping into his arms and covering his face with kisses.

"Thank you, oh, thank you, Alessandro." She burst into tears. "You've made me the happiest woman on earth."

He took the tears in stride. After all, when you were married to the happiest—not to mention the cryingest—woman on earth, you got used to them. "You're welcome, *bella mia.*"

Home is where the heart is, she'd told him repeatedly. Never had the words held such a ring of truth. Emotions filled him, strong, healthy, ungoverned emotions. Emotions he'd never again have trouble expressing.

He laughed out loud. "You know I'm always happy to give you something to cry about."

MILLS & BOON®

Makes any time special™

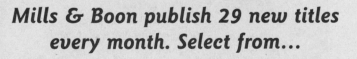

Mills & Boon publish 29 new titles every month. Select from...

Modern Romance™   **Tender Romance**™

Sensual Romance™

Medical Romance™ **Historical Romance**™

MAT2

Together for the first time
3 compelling novels by
bestselling author

PENNY
JORDAN

The
Bride's
BOUQUET

One wedding — one bouquet —
leads to three trips to the altar

Published on 22nd September

MILLS & BOON®

0010/116/MB6

FREE
2 BOOKS
AND A SURPRISE GIFT!

We would like to take this opportunity to thank you for reading this Mills & Boon® book by offering you the chance to take TWO more specially selected titles from the Tender Romance™ series absolutely FREE! We're also making this offer to introduce you to the benefits of the Reader Service™ —

- ★ FREE home delivery
- ★ FREE monthly Newsletter
- ★ FREE gifts and competitions
- ★ Exclusive Reader Service discounts
- ★ Books available before they're in the shops

Accepting these FREE books and gift places you under no obligation to buy; you may cancel at any time, even after receiving your free shipment. Simply complete your details below and return the entire page to the address below. *You don't even need a stamp!*

YES! Please send me 2 free Tender Romance books and a surprise gift. I understand that unless you hear from me, I will receive 4 superb new titles every month for just £2.40 each, postage and packing free. I am under no obligation to purchase any books and may cancel my subscription at any time. The free books and gift will be mine to keep in any case.

N0ZEC

Ms/Mrs/Miss/Mr ....Initials ....

BLOCK CAPITALS PLEASE

Surname ....

Address ....

....

....Postcode ....

Send this whole page to:
UK: FREEPOST CN81, Croydon, CR9 3WZ
EIRE: PO Box 4546, Kilcock, County Kildare (stamp required)